PAGES FROM COLD POINT

Paul Bowles was born in New York and came to Europe in 1931 to study music with Aaron Copland. He has travelled widely. In 1938 he married Jane Auer, herself a gifted novelist and playwright, who was to achieve literary fame. After the war they settled in Tangier, which is now Paul Bowles's permanent home.

'At his best, Bowles has no peer' *Time*

'The extreme beauty of Bowles's writing, his vibrant response to colour and sound, make [him] a "must" to anyone on the watch for outstanding talent' *Sunday Times*

'A superb storyteller' *Life*

'An original and important writer' *Guardian*

'Few writers have Paul Bowles's skill in evocation while making of the familiar something new and extraordinary' *The Times*

Also in Arena by Paul Bowles

LET IT COME DOWN
MIDNIGHT MASS
THE SPIDER'S HOUSE
UP ABOVE THE WORLD

With Mohammed Mrabet

LOVE WITH A FEW HAIRS

PAGES FROM
COLD POINT

and other stories

Paul Bowles

An Arena Book
Published by Arrow Books Limited
62-65 Chandos Place, London WC2N 4NW

An imprint of Century Hutchinson Limited

London Melbourne Sydney Auckland
Johannesburg and agencies throughout
the world

First published in Great Britain by
Peter Owen Limited 1968
Zenith edition 1983
Arena edition 1986
© Paul Bowles 1950, 1951, 1954, 1955, 1957, 1958,
1961, 1962, 1964, 1967

Printed and bound in Great Britain by
The Guernsey Press Co. Ltd, Guernsey, C.I.

ISBN 0 09 950310 7

Contents

Pages from Cold Point

Our civilization is doomed to a short life : its component parts are too heterogeneous. I personally am content to see everything in the process of decay. The bigger the bombs, the quicker it will be done. The world is visually too hideous for one to make the attempt to preserve it. Let it go. Perhaps some day another form of life will come along. Either way, it is of no consequence. At the same time, I am still a part of life, and I am bound by this to protect myself to whatever extent I am able. And so I am here. Here in the Islands vegetation still has the upper hand, and man has to fight even to make his presence seen at all. It is beautiful here, the trade winds blow all year, and I suspect that bombs are extremely unlikely to be wasted on this unfrequented side of the island, if indeed on any part of it.

I was loath to give up the house after Hope's death. But it was the obvious move to make. My university career always having been an utter farce (since I believe no reason inducing a man to 'teach' can possibly be a valid one), I was elated by the idea of resigning, and as soon as her affairs had been settled and the money properly invested, I lost no time in doing so.

I think that week was the first time since childhood that I had managed to recapture the feeling of there being a content in existence. I went from one pleasant house to the next, making my adieux to the English quacks, the

Philosophy fakirs, and so on—even to those colleagues with whom I was merely on speaking terms. I watched the envy in their faces when I announced my departure by Pan American on Saturday morning; and the greatest pleasure I felt in all this was in being able to answer, 'Nothing', when I was asked, as invariably I was, what I intended to 'do'.

When I was a boy people used to refer to Charles as 'Big Brother C', although he is only a scant year older than I. To me now he is merely 'Fat Brother C', a successful lawyer. His thick red face and hands, his back-slapping joviality, and his fathomless hypocritical prudery, these are the qualities which make him truly repulsive to me. There is also the fact that he once looked not unlike the way Racky does now. And after all, he is still my big brother, and disapproves openly of everything I do. The loathing I feel for him is so strong that for years I have not been able to swallow a morsel of food or a drop of liquid in his presence without making a prodigious effort. No one knows this but me—certainly not Charles, who would be the last one I should tell about it. He came up on the late train two nights before I left. He got quickly to the point—as soon as he was settled with a highball.

'So you're off for the wilds,' he said, sitting forward in his chair like a salesman.

'If you can call it the wilds,' I replied. 'Certainly it's not wild like Mitichi.' (He has a lodge in northern Quebec.) 'I consider it really civilized.'

He drank and smacked his lips together stiffly, bringing the glass down hard on his knee.

'And Racky. You're taking him along?'

'Of course.'

'Out of school. Away. So he'll see nobody but you. You think that's good.'

I looked at him. 'I do,' I said.

'By God, if I could stop you legally, I would!' he cried, jumping up and putting his glass on the mantel. I was trembling inwardly with excitement, but I merely sat and watched him. He went on. 'You're not fit to have custody of the kid!' he shouted. He shot a stern glance at me over his spectacles.

'You think not?' I said gently.

Again he looked sharply at me. 'D'ye think I've forgotten?'

I was understandably eager to get him out of the house as soon as I could. As I piled and sorted letters and magazines on the desk, I said : 'Is that all you came to tell me? I have a good deal to do tomorrow and I must get some sleep. I probably shan't see you at breakfast. Agnes'll see that you eat in time to make the early train.'

All he said was : 'God! Wake up! Get wise to yourself! You're not fooling anybody, you know.'

That kind of talk is typical of Charles. His mind is slow and obtuse; he constantly imagines that everyone he meets is playing some private game of deception with him. He is so utterly incapable of following the functioning of even a moderately evolved intellect that he finds the will to secretiveness and duplicity everywhere.

'I haven't time to listen to that sort of nonsense,' I said, preparing to leave the room.

But he shouted : 'You don't want to listen! No! Of course not! You just want to do what you want to do. You just want to go on off down there and live as you've a mind to, and to hell with the consequences!' At this point I heard Racky coming downstairs. C. obviously heard nothing, and he raved on. 'But just remember, I've got your number all right, and if there's any trouble with the boy I'll know who's to blame.'

I hurried across the room and opened the door so he could see that Racky was there in the hallway. That stopped his tirade. It was hard to know whether Racky had heard any of it or not. Although he is not a quiet young person, he is the soul of discretion, and it is almost never possible to know any more about what goes on inside his head than he intends one to know.

I was annoyed that C. should have been bellowing at me in my own house. To be sure, he is the only one from whom I would accept such behavior, but then, no father likes to have his son see him take criticism meekly. Racky simply stood there in his bathrobe, his angelic face quite devoid of expression, saying : 'Tell Uncle Charley good night for me, will you? I forgot.'

I said I would, and quickly shut the door. When I thought Racky was back upstairs in his room, I bade Charles good night. I have never been able to get out of his presence fast enough. The effect he has on me dates from an early period of our lives, from days I dislike to recall.

Racky is a wonderful boy. After we arrived, when we found it impossible to secure a proper house near any town where he might have the company of English boys and girls his own age, he showed no sign of chagrin, although he must have been disappointed. Instead, as we went out of the renting office into the glare of the street, he grinned and said : 'Well, I guess we'll have to get bikes, that's all.'

The few available houses near what Charles would have called 'civilization' turned out to be so ugly and so impos-

sibly confining in atmosphere that we decided immediately
on Cold Point, even though it was across the island and
quite isolated on its seaside cliff. It was beyond a doubt one
of the most desirable properties on the island, and Racky
was as enthusiastic about its splendors as I.

'You'll get tired of being alone out there, just with me,'
I said to him as we walked back to the hotel.

'Aw, I'll get along all right. When do we look for the
bikes?'

At his insistence we bought two the next morning. I was
sure I should not make much use of mine, but I reflected
that an extra bicycle might be convenient to have around
the house. It turned out that all the servants had their own
bicycles, without which they would not have been able to
get to and from the village of Orange Walk, eight miles
down the shore. So for a while I was forced to get astride
mine each morning before breakfast and pedal madly along
beside Racky for a half-hour. We would ride through the
cool early air, under the towering silk-cotton trees near the
house, and out to the great curve in the shoreline where
the waving palms bend landward in the stiff breeze that
always blows there. Then we would make a wide turn and
race back to the house, loudly discussing the degrees of our
desires for the various items of breakfast we knew were
awaiting us there on the terrace. Back home we would eat
in the wind, looking out over the Caribbean, and talk about
the news in yesterday's local paper, brought to us by Isiah
each morning from Orange Walk. Then Racky would disappear for the whole morning on his bicycle, riding furiously
along the road in one direction or the other until he had
discovered an unfamiliar strip of sand along the shore that
he could consider a new beach. At lunch he would describe
it in detail to me, along with a recounting of all the physical

hazards involved in hiding the bicycle among the trees (so that natives passing along the road on foot would not spot it), or in climbing down unscalable cliffs that turned out to be much higher than they had appeared at first sight, or in measuring the depth of the water preparatory to diving from the rocks, or in judging the efficacy of the reef in barring sharks and barracuda.

There is never any element of bragadoccio in Racky's relating of his exploits—only the joyous excitement he derives from telling how he satisfies his inexhaustible curiosity. And his mind shows its alertness in all directions at once. I do not mean to say that I expect him to be an 'intellectual'. That is no affair of mine, nor do I have any particular interest in whether or not he turns out to be a thinking man. I know he will always have a certain boldness of manner and a great purity of spirit in judging values. The former will prevent his becoming what I call a 'victim' : he never will be brutalized by realities. And his unerring sense of balance in ethical considerations will shield him from the paralyzing effects of present-day materialism.

For a boy of sixteen Racky has an extraordinary innocence of vision. I do not say that as a doting father, although God knows I can never even think of the boy without that familiar overwhelming sensation of delight and gratitude for being vouchsafed the privilege of sharing my life with him. What he takes so completely as a matter of course, our daily life here together, is a source of never-ending wonder to me; and I reflect upon it a good part of each day, just sitting here being conscious of my great good fortune in having him all to myself, beyond the reach of prying eyes and malicious tongues. (I suppose I am really thinking of C. when I write that.) And I believe that a part of the charm in sharing Racky's life with him consists pre-

cisely in his taking it all so utterly for granted. I have never
asked him whether he likes being here—it is so patent that
he does, very much. I think if he were to turn to me one day
and tell me how happy he is here, that somehow, perhaps,
the spell might be broken. Yet if he were to be thoughtless
and inconsiderate, or even unkind to me, I feel that I should
be able only to love him the more for it.

I have reread that last sentence. What does it mean?
And why should I even imagine it could mean anything
more than it says?

Still, much as I may try, I can never believe in the gratu-
itous, isolated fact. What I must mean is that I feel that
Racky already has been in some way inconsiderate. But in
what way? Surely I cannot resent his bicycle treks; I cannot expect him to want to stay and sit talking with me all
day. And I never worry about his being in danger; I know
he is more capable than most adults of taking care of himself, and that he is no more likely than any native to come
to harm crawling over the cliffs or swimming in the bays.
At the same time there is no doubt in my mind that something about our existence annoys me. I must resent some
detail in the pattern, whatever that pattern may be. Perhaps
it is just his youth, and I am envious of the lithe body, the
smooth skin, the animal energy and grace.

For a long time this morning I sat looking out to sea, trying
to solve that small puzzle. Two white herons came and
perched on a dead stump, east of the garden. They stayed
a long time there without stirring. I would turn my head
away and accustom my eyes to the bright sea-horizon, then
I would look suddenly at them to see if they had shifted

position, but they would always be in the same attitude. I tried to imagine the black stump without them—a purely vegetable landscape—but it was impossible. All the while I was slowly forcing myself to accept a ridiculous explanation of my annoyance with Racky. It had made itself manifest to me only yesterday, when instead of appearing for lunch, he had sent a young colored boy from Orange Walk to say that he would be lunching in the village. I could not help noticing that the boy was riding Racky's bicycle. I had been waiting lunch a good half hour for him, and I had Gloria serve immediately as the boy rode off, back to the village. I was curious to know in what sort of place and with whom Racky could be eating, since Orange Walk, as far as I know, is inhabited exclusively by Negroes, and I was sure Gloria would be able to shed some light on the matter, but I could scarcely ask her. However, as she brought on the dessert, I said : 'Who was that boy that brought the message from Mister Racky?'

She shrugged her shoulders. 'A young lad of Orange Walk. He's named Wilmot.'

When Racky returned at dusk, flushed from his exertion (for he never rides casually), I watched him closely. His behavior struck my already suspicious eyes as being one of false heartiness and a rather forced good humor. He went to his room early and read for quite a while before turning off his light. I took a long walk in the almost day-bright moonlight, listening to the songs of the night insects in the trees. And I sat for a while in the dark on the stone railing of the bridge across Black River. (It is really only a brook that rushes down over the rocks from the mountain a few miles inland, to the beach near the house.) In the night it always sounds louder and more important than it does in the daytime. The music of the water over the stones relaxed

my nerves, although why I had need of such a thing I find
it difficult to understand, unless I was really upset by
Racky's not having come home to lunch. But if that were true
it would be absurd, and moreover, dangerous—just the sort
of thing the parent of an adolescent has to beware of and
fight against, unless he is indifferent to the prospect of losing
the trust and affection of his offspring permanently. Racky
must stay out whenever he likes, with whom he likes, and
for as long as he likes, and I must not think twice about it,
much less mention it to him, or in any way give the impression of prying. Lack of confidence on the part of a parent
is the one unforgivable sin.

Although we still take our morning dip together on aris-
ing, it is three weeks since we have been for the early spin.
One morning I found that Racky had jumped onto his
bicycle in his wet trunks while I was still swimming, and
gone by himself, and since then there has been an unspoken
agreement between us that such is to be the procedure : he
will go alone. Perhaps I held him back; he likes to ride so
fast.

Young Peter, the smiling gardener from Saint Ives Cove,
is Racky's special friend. It is amusing to see them together
among the bushes, crouched over an ant-hill or rushing
about trying to catch a lizard, almost of an age the two,
yet so disparate—Racky with his tan skin looking nearly
white in contrast to the glistening black of the other. Today
I know I shall be alone for lunch, since it is Peter's day off.
On such days they usually go together on their bicycles into
Saint Ives Cove, where Peter keeps a small rowboat. They
fish along the coast there, but they have never returned with
anything so far.

Meanwhile I am here alone, sitting on the rocks in the
sun, from time to time climbing down to cool myself in the

water, always conscious of the house behind me under the
high palms, like a large glass boat filled with orchids and
lilies. The servants are clean and quiet, and the work seems
to be accomplished almost automatically. The good, black
servants are another blessing of the islands; the British, born
here in this paradise, have no conception of how fortunate
they are. In fact, they do nothing but complain. One must
have lived in the United States to appreciate the wonder of
this place. Still, even here ideas are changing each day.
Soon the people will decide that they want their land to be a
part of today's monstrous world, and once that happens, it
will be all over. As soon as you have that desire, you are
infected with the deadly virus, and you begin to show the
symptoms of the disease. You live in terms of time and
money, and you think in terms of society and progress. Then
all that is left for you is to kill the other people who think
the same way, along with a good many of those who do not,
since that is the final manifestation of the malady. Here
for the moment at any rate, one has a feeling of staticity—
existence ceases to be like those last few seconds in the hour-
glass when what is left of the sand suddenly begins to rush
through to the bottom all at once. For the moment, it seems
suspended. And if it seems, it is. Each wave at my feet, each
bird-call in the forest at my back, does *not* carry me one
step nearer the final disaster. The disaster is certain, but it
will suddenly have happened, that is all. Until then, time
stays still.

I am upset by a letter in this morning's mail : the Royal
Bank of Canada requests that I call in person at its central
office to sign the deposit slips and other papers for a sum

that was cabled from the bank in Boston. Since the central
office is on the other side of the island, fifty miles away, I
shall have to spend the night over there and return the following day. There is no point in taking Racky along. The
sight of 'civilization' might awaken a longing for it in him;
one never knows. I am sure it would have done in me when
I was his age. And if that should once start, he would
merely be unhappy, since there is nothing for him but to
stay here with me, at least for the next two years, when I
hope to renew the lease, or, if things in New York pick up,
buy the place. I am sending word by Isiah, when he goes
home into Orange Walk this evening, to have the McCoigh
car call for me at seven-thirty tomorrow morning. It is an
enormous old open Packard, and Isiah can save the ride out
to work here by piling his bicycle into the back and riding
with McCoigh.

The trip across the island was beautiful, and would have
been highly enjoyable if my imagination had not played
me a strange trick at the very outset. We stopped in Orange
Walk for gasoline, and while that was being seen to, I got
out and went to the corner store for some cigarettes. Since
it was not yet eight o'clock, the store was still closed, and I
hurried up the side street to the other little shop which I
thought might be open. It was, and I bought my cigarettes.
On the way back to the corner I noticed a large black
woman leaning with her arms on the gate in front of her
tiny house, staring into the street. As I passed by her, she
looked straight into my face and said something with the
strange accent of the island. It was said in what seemed an
unfriendly tone, and ostensibly was directed at me, but I

had no notion of what it was. I got back into the car and the driver started it. The sound of the words had stayed in my head, however, as a bright shape outlined by darkness is likely to stay in the mind's eye, in such a way that when one shuts one's eyes one can see the exact contour of the shape. The car was already roaring up the hill toward the overland road when I suddenly reheard the very words. And they were : 'Keep your boy at home, mahn.' I sat perfectly rigid for a moment as the open countryside rushed past. Why should I think she had said that? Immediately I decided that I was giving an arbitrary sense to a phrase I could not have understood even if I had been paying strict attention. And then I wondered why my subconscious should have chosen that sense, since now that I whispered the words over to myself they failed to connect with any anxiety to which my mind might have been disposed. Actually I have never given a thought to Racky's wanderings about Orange Walk. I can find no such preoccupation no matter how I put the question to myself. Then, could she really have said those words? All the way through the mountains I pondered the question, even though it was obviously a waste of energy. And soon I could no longer hear the sound of her voice in my memory : I had played the record over too many times, and worn it out.

Here in the hotel, a gala dance is in progress. The abominable orchestra, comprising two saxophones and one sour violin, is playing directly under my window in the garden, and the serious-looking couples slide about on the waxed concrete floor of the terrace, in the light of strings of paper lanterns. I suppose it is meant to look Japanese.

At this moment I wonder what Racky is doing there in the house with only Peter and Ernest the watchman to keep him company. I wonder if he is asleep. The house, which

I am accustomed to think of as smiling and benevolent in
its airiness, could just as well be in the most sinister and
remote regions of the globe, now that I am here. Sitting with
the absurd orchestra bleating downstairs, I picture it to myself, and it strikes me as terribly vulnerable in its isolation.
In my mind's eye I see the moonlit point with its tall palms
waving restlessly in the wind, its dark cliffs licked by the
waves below. Suddenly, although I struggle against the
sensation, I am inexpressibly glad to be away from the
house, helpless there, far on its point of land, in the silence
of the night. Then I remember that the night is seldom
silent. There are the occasional cries of the night birds, the
droning of the thousands of insects, the loud sea at the
base of the rocks—all the familiar noises that make sleep so
sound. And Racky is there surrounded by them as usual, not
even hearing them. But I feel profoundly guilty for having
left him, unutterably tender and sad at the thought of him,
lying there alone in the house with the two Negroes the
only human beings within miles. If I keep thinking of Cold
Point I shall be more and more nervous.

   I am not going to bed yet. They are all screaming with
laughter down there, the idiots; I could never sleep anyway. The bar is still open. Fortunately it is on the street
side of the hotel. For once I need a few drinks.

Much later, but I feel no better; I may be a little drunk.
The dance is over and it is quiet in the garden, but the room
is too hot.

As I was falling asleep last night, all dressed, and with the
overhead light shining sordidly in my face, I heard the

black woman's voice again, more clearly even than I did in the car yesterday. For some reason this morning there is no doubt in my mind that the words I heard are the words she said. I accept that and go on from there. Suppose she did tell me to keep Racky home. It could only mean that she, or someone else in Orange Walk, has had a childish altercation with him; although I must say it is hard to conceive of Racky's entering into any sort of argument or feud with those people. To set my mind at rest (for I do seem to be taking the whole thing with great seriousness), I am going to stop in the village this afternoon before going home, and try to see the woman. I am extremely curious to know what she could have meant.

I had not been conscious until this evening when I came back to Cold Point how powerful they are, all those physical elements that go to make up its atmosphere : the sea and wind sounds that isolate the house from the road, the brilliancy of the water, sky and sun, the bright colors and strong odors of the flowers, the feeling of space both outside and within the house. One naturally accepts these things when one is living here. This afternoon when I returned I was conscious of them all over again, of their existence and their strength. All of them together are like a powerful drug; coming back made me feel as though I had been disintoxicated and were returning to the scene of my former indulgences. Now at eleven it is as if I had never been absent an hour. Everything is the same as always, even to the dry palm branch that scrapes against the window screen by my night table. And indeed, it is only thirty-six hours since I was here; but I always expect my absence from a place to bring about irremediable changes.

Strangely enough, now that I think of it, I feel that something *has* changed since I left yesterday morning, and that is the general attitude of the servants—their collective aura, so to speak. I noticed that difference immediately upon arriving back, but was unable to define it. Now I see it clearly. The network of common understanding which slowly spreads itself through a well-run household has been destroyed. Each person is by himself now. No unfriendliness, however, that I can see. They all behave with the utmost courtesy, excepting possibly Peter, who struck me as looking unaccustomedly glum when I encountered him in the kitchen after dinner. I meant to ask Racky if he had noticed it, but I forgot, and he went to bed early.

In Orange Walk I made a brief stop, on the pretext to McCoigh that I wanted to see the seamstress in the side street. I walked up and back in front of the house where I had seen the woman, but there was no sign of anyone.

As for my absence, Racky seems to have been perfectly content, having spent most of the day swimming off the rocks below the terrace. The insect sounds are at their height now, the breeze is cooler than usual, and I shall take advantage of these favorable conditions to get a good long night's rest.

Today has been one of the most difficult days of my life. I arose early, we had breakfast at the regular time, and Racky went off in the direction of Saint Ives Cove. I lay in the sun on the terrace for a while, listening to the noises of the household's regime. Peter was all over the property, collecting dead leaves and fallen blossoms in a huge basket, and carrying them off to the compost heap. He appeared to be in an even fouler humor than last night. When he came near to me at one point, on his way down to another part of the garden, I called to him. He set the basket down and stood looking at me; then he walked across the grass toward me slowly—reluctantly, it seemed to me.

'Peter, is everything all right with you?'

'Yes, sir.'

'No trouble at home?'

'Oh, no, sir.'

'Good.'

'Yes, sir.'

He went back to his work. But his face belied his words. Not only did he seem to be in a decidedly unpleasant temper; out here in the sunlight he looked positively ill. However, it was not my concern, if he refused to admit it.

When the heavy heat of the sun reached the unbearable point for me, I got out of my chair and went down the side of the cliff along the series of steps cut there in the rock. A level platform is below, and a diving board, for the water is deep. At each side, the rocks spread out and the waves break over them, but by the platform the wall of rock is vertical and the water merely hits against it below the springboard. The place is a tiny amphitheatre, quite cut off in sound and sight from the house. There too, I like to lie in the sun; when I climb out of the water I often remove my trunks and lie stark naked on the springboard. I regularly make fun of Racky because he is embarrassed to do the same. Occasionally he will do it, but never without being coaxed. I was spread out there without a stitch on, being lulled by the slapping of the water, when an unfamiliar voice very close to me said : 'Mister Norton?'

I jumped with nervousness, nearly fell off the spring-board, and sat up, reaching at the same time, but in vain, for my trunks, which were lying on the rock practically at the feet of a middle-aged mulatto gentleman. He was in a white duck suit, and wore a high collar with a black tie, and it seemed to me that he was eyeing me with a certain degree of horror.

My next reaction was one of anger at being trespassed upon in this way. I rose and got the trunks; however, donning them calmly and saying nothing more meaningful than : 'I didn't hear you come down the steps.'

'Shall we go up?' said my caller. As he led the way, I had a definite premonition that he was here on an unpleasant errand. On the terrace we sat down, and he offered me an American cigarette which I did not accept.

'This is a delightful spot,' he said, glancing out to sea and then at the end of his cigarette, which was only partially aglow. He puffed at it.

I said : 'Yes,' waiting for him to go on; presently he did.

'I am from the constabulary of this parish. The police, you see.' And seeing my face, 'This is a friendly call. But still it must be taken as a warning, Mister Norton. It is very serious. If anyone else comes to you about this it will mean trouble for you, heavy trouble. That's why I want to see you privately this way and warn you personally. You see.'

I could not believe I was hearing his words. At length I said faintly : 'But what about?'

'This is not an official call. You must not be upset. I have taken it upon myself to speak to you because I want to save you deep trouble.'

'But I *am* upset!' I cried, finding my voice at last. 'How can I help being upset, when I don't know what you're talking about?'

He moved his chair closer to mine, and spoke in a very low voice.

'I have waited until the young man was away from the house so we could talk in private. You see, it is about him.'

Somehow that did not surprise me. I nodded.

'I will tell you very briefly. The people here are simple country folk. They make trouble easily. Right now they are all talking about the young man you have living here with you. He is your son, I hear.' His inflection here was sceptical.

'Certainly he's my son.'

His expression did not change, but his voice grew indignant. 'Whoever he is, that is a bad young man.'

'What do you mean?' I cried, but he cut in hotly: 'He may be your son; he may not be. I don't care who he is. That is not my affair. But he is bad through and through. We don't have such things going on here, sir. The people in Orange Walk and Saint Ives Cove are very cross now. You don't know what these folk do when they are aroused.'

I thought it my turn to interrupt. 'Please tell me why you say my son is bad. What has he done?' Perhaps the earnestness in my voice reached him, for his face assumed a gentler aspect. He leaned still closer to me and almost whispered.

'He has no shame. He does what he pleases with all the young boys, and the men too, and gives them a shilling so they won't tell about it. But they talk. Of course they talk. Every man for twenty miles up and down the coast knows about it. And the women too, they know about it.' There was a silence.

I had felt myself preparing to get to my feet for the past few seconds because I wanted to go into my room and be alone, to get away from that scandalized stage whisper. I

think I mumbled 'Good morning' or 'Thank you' as I turned
away and began walking toward the house. But he was still
beside me, still whispering like an eager conspirator into
my ear: 'Keep him home, Mister Norton. Or send him
away to school, if he is your son. But make him stay out of
these towns. For his own sake.'

I shook hands with him and went to lie on my bed. From
there I heard his car door slam, heard him drive off. I was
painfully trying to formulate an opening sentence to use in
speaking to Racky about this, feeling that the opening sentence would define my stand. The attempt was merely a
sort of therapeutic action, to avoid thinking about the thing
itself. Every attitude seemed impossible. There was no way
to broach the subject. I suddenly realized that I should
never be able to speak to him directly about it. With the
advent of this news he had become another person—an
adult, mysterious and formidable. To be sure, it did occur
to me that the mulatto's story might not be true, but automatically I rejected the doubt. It was as if I wanted to believe it, almost as if I had already known it, and he had
merely confirmed it.

Racky returned at midday, panting and grinning. The
inevitable comb appeared and was used on the sweaty, un-
ruly locks. Sitting down to lunch, he exclaimed: 'Wow!
What a beach I found this morning! But what a job to get
down to it!' I tried to look unconcerned as I met his gaze;
it was as if our positions had been reversed, and I were
hoping to stem his rebuke. He prattled on about thorns and
vines and his machete. Throughout the meal I kept telling
myself: 'Now is the moment. You must say something.'
But all I said was: 'More salad? Or do you want dessert
now?' So the lunch passed and nothing happened. After I
had finished my coffee I went into my bedroom and looked

at myself in the large mirror. I saw my eyes trying to give
their reflected brothers a little courage. As I stood there I
heard a commotion in the other wing of the house : voices,
bumpings, the sound of a scuffle. Above the noise came
Gloria's sharp voice, imperious and excited : 'No, mahn !
Don't strike him !' And louder : 'Peter, mahn, no !'

I went quickly toward the kitchen, where the trouble
seemed to be, but on the way I was run into by Racky,
who staggered into the hallway with his hands in front of
his face.

'What is it, Racky?' I cried.

He pushed past me into the living room without moving
his hands away from his face; I turned and followed him.
From there he went into his own room, leaving the door
open behind him. I heard him in the bathroom running the
water. I was undecided what to do. Suddenly Peter
appeared in the hall doorway, his hat in his hand. When
he raised his head, I was surprised to see that his cheek
was bleeding. In his eyes was a strange, confused expression of transient fear and deep hostility. He looked down
again.

'May I please talk with you, sir?'

'What was all the racket? What's been happening?'

'May I talk with you outside, sir?' He said it doggedly,
still not looking up.

In view of the circumstances, I humored him. We walked
slowly up the cinder road to the main highway, across the
bridge, and through the forest while he told me his story.
I said nothing.

At the end he said : 'I never wanted to, sir, even the first
time, but after the first time I was afraid, and Mister Racky
was after me every day.'

I stood still, and finally said : 'If you had only told me

this the first time it happened, it would have been much better for everyone.'

He turned his hat in his hands, studying it intently. 'Yes, sir. But I didn't know what everyone was saying about him in Orange Walk until today. You know I always go to the beach at Saint Ives Cove with Mister Racky on my free days. If I had known what they were all saying I wouldn't have been afraid, sir. And I wanted to keep on working here. I needed the money.' Then he repeated what he had already said three times. 'Mister Racky said you'd see about it that I was put in the jail. I'm a year older than Mister Racky, sir.'

'I know, I know,' I said impatiently; and deciding that severity was what Peter expected of me at this point I added : 'You had better get your things together and go home. You can't work here any longer, you know.'

The hostility in his face assumed terrifying proportions as he said : 'If you killed me I would not work any more at Cold Point, sir.'

I turned and walked briskly back to the house, leaving him standing there in the road. It seems he returned at dusk, a little while ago, and got his belongings.

In his room Racky was reading. He had stuck some adhesive tape on his chin and over his cheekbone.

'I've dismissed Peter,' I announced. 'He hit you, didn't he?'

He glanced up. His left eye was swollen, but not yet black.

'He sure did. But I landed him one, too. And I guess I deserved it anyway.'

I rested against the table. 'Why?' I asked nonchalantly.

'Oh, I had something on him from a long time back that he was afraid I'd tell you.'

'And just now you threatened to tell me?'

'Oh, no! He said he was going to quit the job here, and I told him he was yellow.'

'Why did he want to quit? I thought he liked the job.'

'Well, he did, I guess, but he didn't like me.' Racky's candid gaze betrayed a shade of pique. I still leaned against the table.

I persisted. 'But I thought you two got on fine together. You seemed to.'

'Nah. He was just scared of losing his job. I had something on him. He was a good guy, though. I liked him all right.' He paused. 'Has he gone yet?' A strange quaver crept into his voice as he said the last words, and I understood that for the first time Racky's heretofore impeccable histrionics were not quite equal to the occasion. He was very much upset at losing Peter.

'Yes, he's gone,' I said shortly. 'He's not coming back, either.' And as Racky, hearing the unaccustomed inflection in my voice, looked up at me suddenly with faint astonishment in his young eyes, I realized that this was the moment to press on, to say: 'What did you have on him?' But as if he had arrived at the same spot in my mind a fraction of a second earlier, he proceeded to snatch away my advantage by jumping up, bursting into loud song, and pulling off all his clothes. As he stood before me naked, singing at the top of his lungs, and stepped into his swimming trunks, I was conscious that again I should be incapable of saying to him what I must say.

He was in and out of the house all afternoon: some of the time he read in his room, and most of the time he was down on the diving board. It is strange behavior for him; if I could only know what is in his mind. As evening approached, my problem took on a purely obsessive character. I walked to and fro in my room, always pausing at one

end to look out the window over the sea, and at the other
end to glance at my face in the mirror. As if that could
help me! Then I took a drink. And another. I thought I
might be able to do it at dinner, when I felt fortified by
the whiskey. But no. Soon he will have gone to bed. It is
not that I expect to confront him with any accusations.
That I know I never can do. But I must find a way to keep
him from his wanderings, and I must invent a reason to
give him, so that he will never suspect that I know.

We fear for the future of our offspring. It is ludicrous, but
only a little more palpably so than most things in life. A
length of time has passed—days which I am content to
have known, even if now they are over. I think that this
period was what I had always been waiting for life to offer,
the recompense I had unconsciously but firmly expected, in
return for having been held so closely in the grip of existence
all these years.

That evening seems long ago only because I have recalled
its details so many times that they have taken on the color
of legend. Actually my problem already had been solved for
me then, but I did not know it. Because I could not perceive
the pattern, I foolishly imagined that I must cudgel my
brains to find the right words with which to approach
Racky. But it was he who came to me. That same evening,
as I was about to go out for a solitary stroll which I thought
might help me hit upon a formula, he appeared at my door.

'Going for a walk?' he asked, seeing the stick in my hand.

The prospect of making an exit immediately after speaking with him made things seem simpler. 'Yes,' I said, 'but
I'd like to have a word with you first.'

'Sure. What?' I did not look at him because I did not want to see the watchful light I was sure was playing in his eyes at this moment. As I spoke I tapped with my stick along the designs made by the tiles in the floor. 'Racky, would you like to go back to school?'

'Are you kidding? You know I hate school.'

I glanced up at him. 'No, I'm not kidding. Don't look so horrified. You'd probably enjoy being with a bunch of fellows your own age.' (That was not one of the arguments I had meant to use.)

'I might like to be with guys my own age, but I don't want to have to be in school to do it. I've had school enough.'

I went to the door and said lamely: 'I thought I'd get your reactions.'

He laughed, 'No, thanks.'

'That doesn't mean you're not going,' I said over my shoulder as I went out.

On my walk I pounded the highway's asphalt with my stick, stood on the bridge having dramatic visions which involved such eventualities as our moving back to the States, Racky's having a bad spill on his bicycle and being paralyzed for some months, and even the possibility of my letting events take their course, which would doubtless mean my having to visit him now and then in the governmental prison with gifts of food, if it meant nothing more tragic and violent. 'But none of these things will happen,' I said to myself, and I knew I was wasting precious time; he must not return to Orange Walk tomorrow.

I went back toward the point at a snail's pace. There was no moon, and very little breeze. As I approached the house, trying to tread lightly on the cinders so as not to awaken the watchful Ernest and have to explain to him that it was

only I, I saw that there were no lights in Racky's room. The
house was dark save for the dim lamp on my night table. Instead of going in, I skirted the entire building, colliding with
bushes and getting my face sticky with spider webs, and
went to sit a while on the terrace where there seemed to be
a breath of air. The sound of the sea was far out on the reef,
where the breakers sighed. Here below, there were only
slight watery chugs and gurgles now and then. It was an
unusually low tide. I smoked three cigarettes mechanically,
having ceased even to think, and then, my mouth tasting
bitter from the smoke, I went inside.

My room was airless. I flung my clothes onto a chair and
looked at the night table to see if the carafe of water was
there. Then my mouth opened. The top sheet of my bed had
been stripped back to the foot. There on the far side of
the bed, dark against the whiteness of the lower sheet, lay
Racky asleep on his side, and naked.

I stood looking at him for a long time, probably holding
my breath, for I remember feeling a little dizzy at one point.
I was whispering to myself, as my eyes followed the curve
of his arm, shoulder, back, thigh, leg: 'A child. A child.'
Destiny, when one perceives it clearly from very near, has
no qualities at all. The recognition of it and the consciousness of the vision's clarity leave no room on the mind's
horizon. Finally I turned off the light and softly lay down.
The night was absolutely black.

He stayed perfectly quiet until dawn. I shall never know
whether or not he was really asleep all that time. Of course
he couldn't have been, and yet he lay so still. Warm and
firm, but still as death. The darkness and silence were heavy
around us. As the birds began to sing, I sank into a soft,
enveloping slumber; when I awoke in the sunlight later, he
was gone.

I found him down by the water, cavorting alone on the springboard; for the first time, he had discarded his trunks without my suggesting it. All day we stayed together around the terrace and on the rocks, talking, swimming, reading, and just lying flat in the hot sun. Nor did he return to his room when night came. Instead, after the servants were asleep, we brought three bottles of champagne in and set the pail on the night table.

Thus it came about that I was able to touch on the delicate subject that still preoccupied me, and profiting by the new understanding between us, I made my request in the easiest, most natural fashion.

'Racky, would you do me a tremendous favor if I asked you?'

He lay on his back, his hands beneath his head. It seemed to me his regard was circumspect, wanting in candor.

'I guess so,' he said. 'What is it?'

'Will you stay around the house for a few days—a week, say? Just to please me? We can take some rides together, as far as you like. Would you do that for me?'

'Sure thing,' he said, smiling.

I was temporizing, but I was desperate.

Perhaps a week later—(it is only when one is not fully happy that one is meticulous about time, so that it may have been more, or less)—we were having breakfast. Isiah stood by in the shade, waiting to pour us more coffee.

'I noticed you had a letter from Uncle Charley the other day,' said Racky. 'Don't you think we ought to invite him down?'

My heart began to beat with great force.

'Here? He'd hate it here,' I said casually. 'Besides, there's no room. Where would he sleep?' Even as I heard myself

saying the words, I knew that they were the wrong ones,
and that I was not really participating in the conversation.
Again I felt the fascination of complete helplessness that
comes when one is suddenly a conscious onlooker at the
shaping of one's fate.

'In my room,' said Racky. 'It's empty.'

I could see more of the pattern at that moment than I
had ever suspected existed. 'Nonsense,' I said. 'This is not
the sort of place for Uncle Charley.'

Racky appeared to be hitting on an excellent idea. 'Maybe
if I wrote and invited him,' he suggested, motioning to Isiah
for more coffee.

'Nonsense,' I said again, watching still more of the pattern
reveal itself, like a photographic print becoming constantly
clearer in a tray of developing solution.

Isiah filled Racky's cup and returned to the shade. Racky
drank slowly, pretending to be savoring the coffee.

'Well, it won't do any harm to try. He'd appreciate the
invitation,' he said speculatively.

For some reason, at this juncture I knew what to say, and
as I said it, I knew what I was going to do.

'I thought we might fly over to Havana for a few days
next week.'

He looked guardedly interested, and then he broke into a
wide grin. 'Great!' he cried. 'Why wait until next week?'

The next morning the servants called 'Good-bye' to us as
we drove up the cinder road in the McCoigh car. We took
off from the airport at six that evening. Racky was in high
spirits; he kept the stewardess engaged in conversation all
the way to Camagüey.

He was delighted with Havana. Sitting in the bar at the Nacional, we continued to discuss the possibility of having C. pay us a visit at the island. It was not without difficulty that I eventually managed to persuade Racky that writing him would be inadvisable.

We decided to look for an apartment right there in Vedado for Racky. He did not seem to want to come back to Cold Point. We also decided that living in Havana he would need a larger income than I. I am already having the greater part of Hope's estate transferred to his name in the form of a trust fund which I shall administer until he is of age. It was his mother's money, after all.

We bought a new convertible, and he drove me out to Rancho Boyeros in it when I took my plane. A Cuban named Claudio with very white teeth, whom Racky had met in the pool that morning, sat between us.

We were waiting in front of the landing field. An official finally unhooked the chain to let the passengers through. 'If you get fed up, come to Havana,' said Racky, pinching my arm.

The two of them stood together behind the rope, waving to me, their shirts flapping in the wind as the plane started to move.

The wind blows by my head; between each wave there are thousands of tiny licking and chopping sounds as the water hurries out of the crevices and holes; and a part-floating, part-submerged feeling of being in the water haunts my mind even as the hot sun burns my face. I sit here and I read, and I wait for the pleasant sensation of repletion that follows a good meal, to turn slowly, as the hours pass along, into the even more delightful, slightly stirring emotion deep within, which accompanies the awakening of the appetite.

I am perfectly happy here in reality, because I believe that nothing very drastic is likely to befall this part of the island in the near future.

The Time of Friendship

The trouble had been growing bigger each year, ever since the end of the war. From the beginning, although aware of its existence, Fräulein Windling had determined to pay it no attention. At first there were only whispered reports of mass arrests. People said: 'Many thousands of Moslems have been sent to prison in France'. Soon some of her own friends had begun to disappear, like young Bachir and Omar ben Lakhdar, the postmaster of Timimoun, who suddenly one morning were gone, or so she was told, for when she returned the following winter they were not there, and she never had seen them since. The people simply made their faces blank when she tried to talk about it. After the hostilities had begun in earnest, even though the nationalists had derailed the trains and disrupted the trans-Saharan truck service on several occasions, still it was possible to get beyond the disturbed region to her oasis. There in the south the fighting was far away, and the long hours of empty desert that lay between made it seem much farther, almost as though it had been across the sea. If the men of her oasis should ever be infected by the virus of discontent from the far-off north—and this seemed to her almost inconceivable —then in spite of the fact that she was certain that war could bring them nothing but unhappiness, she would have no recourse but to hope for their victory. It was their own land they would be fighting for, their own lives they would be losing in order to win the fight. In the meantime people did not talk; life was hard but peaceful. Each one was aware of the war that was going on in the north, and each one was glad it was far away.

Summers, Fräulein Windling taught in the Freiluftschule in Bern, where she entertained her pupils with tales of the life led by the people in the great desert in Africa. In the village where she lived, she told them, everything was made by the people themselves out of what the desert had to offer. They lived in a world of objects fashioned out of baked earth, woven grass, palmwood and animal skins. There was no metal. Although she did not admit it to the children, this was no longer wholly true, since recently the women had taken to using empty oil tins for carrying water, instead of the goathide bags of a few years before. She had tried to discourage her friends among the village women from this innovation, telling them that the tins could poison the water; they had agreed, and gone on using them. 'They are lazy,' she decided. 'The oil tins are easier to carry.'

When the sun went down and the cool air from the oasis below with its sting of woodsmoke rose to the level of the hotel, she would smell it inside her room and stop whatever she was doing. Then she would put on her burnoose and climb the stairs to the roof. The blanket she lay on while she sunbathed each morning would be there, and she would stretch out on it facing the western sky, and feel the departed sun's heat still strong underneath her body. It was one of the great pleasures of the day, to watch the light changing in the oasis below, when dusk and the smoke from the evening fires slowly blotted out the valley. There always came a moment when all that was left was the faint outline, geometric and precise, of the mass of mud prisms that was the village, and a certain clump of high date palms that stood outside its entrance. The houses themselves were no longer there, and eventually the highest palm disappeared; and unless there was a moon all that remained to be seen was the dying sky, the sharp edges of the rocks on the *hammada*, and a blank expanse of mist that lay over the valley but did not reach as far up the cliffs as the hotel.

Perhaps twice each winter a group of the village women would invite Fräulein Windling to go with them up into the vast land of the dunes to look for firewood. The glare here was cruel. There was not even the trace of a twig or a stem anywhere on the sand, yet as they wandered along the crests barefoot the women could spot the places where roots lay buried beneath the surface, and then they would stoop, uncover them, and dig them up. 'The wind leaves a sign,' they told her, but she was never certain of being able to identify the sign, nor could she understand how there might be a connection between the invisible roots in the sand and the wind in the air above. 'What we have lost, they still possess,' she thought.

Her first sight of the desert and its people had been a transfiguring experience; indeed, it seemed to her now that before coming here she had never been in touch with life at all. She believed firmly that each day she spent here increased the aggregate of her resistance. She coveted the rugged health of the natives, when her own was equally strong, but because she was white and educated, she was convinced that her body was intrinsically inferior.

All the work in the hotel was done by one quiet, sad-faced man named Boufelja. He had been there when she had first arrived many years ago; for Fräulein Windling he had come to be as much a part of the place as the cliffs across the valley. She often sat on at her table by the fireplace after lunch, playing cards by herself, until the logs no longer

gave out heat. There were two very young French soldiers
from the fort opposite, who ate in the hotel dining-room.
They drank a great amount of wine, and it annoyed her to
see their faces slowly turning red as they sat there. At first
the soldiers had tipped their caps to her as they went out,
and they had stopped their laughing long enough to say,
'*Bonjour, madame,*' to her, but now they no longer did. She
was happy when they had left, and savored the moment
before the fire burned out, while it still glowed under the
gusts of wind that wandered down the wide chimney.

Almost always the wind sprang up early in the afternoon,
a steady, powerful blowing that roared through the thousands of palms in the oasis below and howled under each
door in the hotel, covering the more distant village sounds.
This was the hour when she played solitaire, or merely sat,
watching the burnt-out logs as they fell to pieces before her
eyes. Later she would go along the terrace, a high, bright
place like the deck of a great ship sailing through the desert
afternoon, hurrying into her room for an instant to get her
sweater and cane, and start out on a walk. Sometimes she
went southward following the river valley, along the foot
of the silent cliffs and through the crooked gorges, to an
abandoned village built in a very hot place at a turn in the
canyon. The sheer walls of rock behind it sent back the heat,
so that the air burned her throat as she breathed it in. Or
she went farther, to where the cliff dwellings were, with
their animals and symbols incised in the rock.

Returning along the road that led to the village, deep in
the green shade of the thickest part of the palm forest, she
was regularly aware of the same group of boys sitting at the
turn of the road, at a place just before it led up the hill to
the shops and the village. They squatted on the sand behind
the feathery branches of a giant tamarisk, quietly talking.

When she came up to them she greeted them, and they always replied, remained silent a moment until she had passed by, and then resumed their conversation. As far as she could tell, there was never any reference to her by word, and yet this year it sometimes seemed to her that once she had gone by, their inflection had subtly altered, as though there had been a modulation into another key. Did their attitude border on derision? She did not know, but since this was the first time during all her years in the desert that the idea had ever suggested itself to her, she put it resolutely out of her mind. 'A new generation requires a new technique if one is to establish contact,' she thought. 'It is for me to find it.' Nevertheless she was sorry that there was no other way of getting into the village save along this main road where they invariably gathered. Even the slight tension caused by having to go past them marred the pleasure of her walks.

One day she realized with a slight shock of shame that she did not even know what the boys looked like. She had seen them only as a group from a distance; when she drew near enough to say good-day to them, she always had her head down, watching the road. The fact that she had been afraid to look at them was unacceptable; now, as she came up to them, she stared into the eyes of one after the other, carefully. Nodding gravely, she went on. Yes, they were insolent faces, she thought—not at all like the faces of their elders. The respectful attitudes into which they had been startled were the crudest sort of shamming. But the important thing to her was that she had won: she was no longer preoccupied with having to pass by them every day. Slowly she even grew to recognize each boy.

There was one, she noted, younger than the others, who always sat a little apart from them, and it was this shy one

who stood talking to Boufelja in the hotel kitchen early
one morning when she went in. She pretended not to notice
him. 'I am going to my room to work on the machine for
about an hour,' she told Boufelja. 'You can come then to
make up the room,' and she turned to go out. As she went
through the doorway she glanced at the boy's face. He was
looking at her, and he did not turn away when his eyes met
hers. 'How are you?' she said. Perhaps half an hour later,
when she was typing her second letter, she raised her head.
The boy was standing on the terrace looking at her through
the open door. He squinted, for the wind was strong; behind
his head she saw the tops of the palms bending.

'If he wants to watch, let him watch,' she said to herself,
deciding to pay him no attention. After a while he went
away. While Boufelja served her lunch, she questioned him
about the boy. 'Like an old man,' said Boufelja. 'Twelve
years old but very serious. Like some old, old man.' He
smiled, then shrugged. 'It's the way God wanted him to be.'

'Of course,' she said, remembering the boy's alert, unhappy face. 'A young dog that everyone has kicked,' she
thought, 'but he hasn't given up.'

In the days that followed, he came often to the terrace
and stood watching her while she typed. Sometimes she
waved to him, or said : 'Good morning.' Without answering
he would take a step backward, so that he was out of her
range. Then he would continued to stand where he was.
His behavior irked her, and one day when he had done
this, she quickly got up and went to the door. 'What is it?'
she asked him, trying to smile as she spoke.

'I didn't do anything,' he said, his eyes reproachful.

'I know,' she answered. 'Why don't you come in?'

The boy looked swiftly around the terrace as if for help;
then he bowed his head and stepped inside the door. Here

he stood waiting, his head down, looking miserable. From her luggage she brought out a bag of hard candy, and handed him a piece. Then she put a few simple questions to him, and found that his French was much better than she had expected. 'Do the other boys know French as well as you?' she asked him.

'*Non, madame,*' he said, shaking his head slowly. 'My father used to be a soldier. Soldiers speak good French.'

She tried to keep her face from expressing the disapproval she felt, for she despised everything military. 'I see,' she said with some asperity, turning back to her table and shuffling the papers. 'Now I must work,' she told him, immediately adding in a warmer voice, 'but you come back tomorrow, if you like.' He waited an instant, looking at her with unchanged wistfulness. Then slowly he smiled, and laid the candy wrapper, folded into a tiny square, on the corner of her table. '*Au revoir, madame,*' he said, and went out of the door. In the silence she heard the scarcely audible thud of his bare heels on the earth floor of the terrace. 'In this cold,' she thought. 'Poor child! If I ever buy anything for him it will be a pair of sandals.'

Each day thereafter, when the sun was high enough to give substance to the still morning air, the boy would come stealthily along the terrace to her door, stand a few seconds, and then say in a lost voice that was all the smaller and more hushed for the great silence outside : '*Bonjour, madame.*' She would tell him to come in, and they would shake hands gravely, he afterward raising the backs of his fingers to his lips, always with the same slow ceremoniousness. She sometimes tried to fathom his countenance as he went through this ritual, to see if by any chance she could detect a shade of mockery there; instead she saw an expression of devotion so convincing that it startled her, and she looked away quickly. She always kept a bit of bread or some biscuits in a drawer of the wardrobe; when she had brought the food out and he was eating it, she would ask him for news about the families in his quarter of the village. For discipline's sake she offered him a piece of candy only every other day. He sat on the floor by the doorway, on a torn old camel blanket, and he watched her constantly, never turning his head away from her.

She wanted to know what he was called, but she was aware of how secretive the inhabitants of the region were about names, seldom giving their true ones to strangers; this was a peculiarity she respected because she knew it had its roots in their own prehistoric religion. So she forebore asking him, sure that the time would come when he trusted her enough to give it of his own volition. And the moment happened one morning unexpectedly, when he had just recounted several legends involving the great Moslem king of long ago, whose name was Solomon. Suddenly he stopped, and forcing himself to gaze steadily at her without blinking, he said : 'And my name too is Slimane, the same as the king.'

She tried to teach him to read, but he did not seem able to learn. Often just as she felt he was about to connect two loose ends of ideas and perhaps at last make a contact which would enable him to understand the principle, a look of resignation and passivity would appear in his face, and he would willfully cut off the stream of effort from its source, and remain sitting, merely looking at her, shaking his head from side to side to show that it was useless. It was hard not to lose patience with him at such moments.

The following year she decided not to go on with the lessons, and to use Slimane instead as a guide, bearer and companion, a role which she immediately saw was more

suited to his nature than that of pupil. He did not mind how
far they went or how much equipment he had to carry; on
the contrary, to him a long excursion was that much more
of an event, and whatever she loaded onto him he bore with
the air of one upon whom an honor is conferred. It was
probably her happiest season in the desert, that winter of
comradeship when together they made the countless pilgrim-
ages down the valley. As the weeks passed the trips grew in
scope, and the hour of departure was brought forward until
it came directly after she had finished her breakfast. All day
long, trudging in the open sun and in the occasional shade
of the broken fringe of palms that skirted the river-bed, she
conversed passionately with him. Sometimes she could see
that he felt like telling her what was in his head, and she
let him speak for as long as his enthusiasm lasted, often
reviving it at the end with carefully chosen questions. But
usually it was she who did the speaking as she walked behind him. Pounding the stony ground with her steel-tipped
stick each time her right foot went down, she told him in
great detail the story of the life of Hitler, showing why he
was hated by the Christians. This she thought necessary
since Slimane had been under a different impression, and
indeed had imagined that the Europeans thought as highly
of the vanished leader as did he and the rest of the people
in the village. She talked a good deal about Switzerland,
casually stressing the cleanliness, honesty and good health
of her countrymen in short parables of daily life. She told
him about Jesus, Martin Luther and Garibaldi, taking care
to keep Jesus distinct from the Moslem prophet Sidna Aissa,
since even for the sake of argument she could not agree for
an instant with the Islamic doctrine according to which the
Savior was a Moslem. Slimane's attitude of respect bordering on adoration with regard to her never altered unless she

inadvertently tangled with the subject of Islam; then, no matter what she said (for at that point it seemed that automatically he was no longer within hearing) he would shake his head interminably and cry : 'No, no, no, no! Nazarenes know nothing about Islam. Don't talk, madame, I beg you, because you don't know what you're saying. No, no, no!'

Long ago she had kept the initial promise to herself that she would buy him sandals; this purchase had been followed by others. At fairly regular intervals she had taken him to Benaissa's store to buy a shirt, a pair of baggy black cotton trousers of the kind worn by the Chaamba camel-drivers, and ultimately a new white burnoose, despite the fact that she knew the entire village would discuss the giving of so valuable an object. She also knew that it was only the frequent bestowing of such gifts that kept Slimane's father from forbidding him to spend his time with her. Even so, according to reports brought by Slimane, he sometimes objected. But Slimane himself, she was sure, wanted nothing, expected nothing.

It was each year when March was drawing to a close that the days began to be painfully hot and even the nights grew breathless; then, although it always required a strenuous effort of the will to make herself take the step which would bring about renewed contact with the outside world, she would devote two or three days to washing her clothing and preparing for the journey. When the week set for her departure had come, she went over to the fort and put in a call to the café at Kerzaz, asking the proprietor to tell the driver of the next northbound truck to take the detour that would enable her to catch him at a point only about three kilometres from the village.

She and Slimane had come back to the hotel on the afternoon of their last excursion down the valley; Fräulein Wind-

ling stood on the terrace looking out at the orange mountains of sand behind the fort. Slimane had taken the packs
into the room and put them down. She turned and said:
'Bring the big tin box.' When he had pulled it out from
under the bed he carried it to her, dusting it off with the
sleeve of his shirt, and she led the way up the stairs to the
roof. They sat down on the blanket; the glow of the vanished
sun's furnace heated their faces. A few flies still hovered,
now and then attacking their necks. Slimane handed her the
biscuit tin and she gave him a fistful of chocolate-covered
cakes. 'So many all at once?'

'Yes,' she said. 'You know I'm going home in four days.'

He looked down at the blanket a moment before reply-
ing. 'I know,' he murmured. He was silent again. Then he
cried out aggrievedly: 'Boufelja says it's hot here in the
summer. It's not hot! In our house it's cool. It's like
the oasis where the big pool is. You would never be hot
there.'

'I have to earn money. You know that. I want to come
back next year.'

He said sadly: 'Next year, madame! Only Moulana
knows how next year will be.'

Some camels growled as they rolled in the sand at the
foot of the fort; the light was receding swiftly. 'Eat your
biscuits,' she told him, and she ate one herself. 'Next year
we'll go to Abadla with the caid, *incha'Allah*.'

He sighed deeply. 'Ah, madame!' he said. She noted, at
first with a pang of sympathy and then, reconsidering, with
disapproval, the anguish that lent his voice its unaccustomed
intensity. It was the quality she least liked in him, this
faintly theatrical self-pity. 'Next year you'll be a man,' she
told him firmly. Her voice grew less sure, assumed a hope-
ful tone. 'You'll remember all the things we talked about?'

She sent him a postcard from Marseille, and showed her classes photographs they had taken of one another, and of the caid. The children were impressed by the caid's voluminous turban. 'Is he a Bedouin?' asked one.

When she left the embassy office she knew that this was the last year she would be returning to the desert. There was not only the official's clearly expressed unfriendliness and suspicion : for the first time he had made her answer a list of questions which she found alarming. He wanted to know what subjects she taught in the Freiluftschüle, whether she had ever been a journalist, and exactly where she proposed to be each day after arriving in the Sahara. She had almost retorted : 'I go where I feel like going. I don't make plans.' But she had merely named the oasis. She knew that Frenchmen had no respect for elderly Swiss ladies who wore woolen stockings; this simply made them more contemptible in her eyes. However, it was they who controlled the Sahara.

The day the ship put into the African port it was raining. She knew the gray terraced ramps of the city were there in the gloom ahead, but they were invisible. The ragged European garments of the dock workers were soaked with rain. Later, the whole rain-sodden city struck her as grim, and the people passing along the streets looked unhappy. The change, even from the preceding year, was enormous; it made her sad to sit in the big, cold café where she went for coffee after dinner, and so she returned to her hotel and slept. The next day she got on the train for Perrégaux. The rain fell most of the day. In Perrégaux she took a room in a hotel near the station, and stayed in it, listening to the rain rattle down the gutter by her window. 'This place would be a convenient model for Hell,' she wrote to a friend in Basel before going to sleep that night. 'A full-blown example of the social degeneracy achieved by forced cultural hybridism.

Populace debased and made hostile by generations of merciless exploitation. I take the southbound narrow-gauge train tomorrow morning for a happier land, and trust that my friend the sun will appear at some point during the day. *Seien Sie herzlich gegrüsst von Ihrer Maria.*'

At the train crawled southward, up over the high plateau land, the clouds were left behind and the sun took charge of the countryside. Fräulein Windling sat attentively by the smeared window, enveloped in an increasing sadness. As long as it had been raining, she had imagined the rain as the cause of her depression : the gray cloud light gave an unaccustomed meaning to the landscape by altering forms and distances. Now she understood that the more familiar and recognizable the contours of the desert were to become, the more conscious she would be of having no reason to be in it, because it was her last visit.

Two days later, when the truck stopped to let her out, Boufelja stood in the sun beside the boulders waving; one of the men of the village was with him to help carry the luggage. Once the truck had gone and its cloud of yellow dust had fled across the *hammada*, the silence was there; it seemed that no sound could be louder than the crunch of their shoes on the ground.

'How is Slimane?' she asked. Boufelja was noncommittal. 'He's all right,' he said. 'They say he tried to run away. But he didn't get very far.' The report might be true, or it might be false; in any case she determined not to allude to it unless Slimane himself mentioned it first.

She felt an absurd relief when they came to the edge of the cliffs and she saw the village across the valley. Not until she had made the rounds of the houses where her friends lived, discussed their troubles with them and left some pills here and some candy there, was she convinced that no important change had come to the oasis during her absence. She went to the house of Slimane's parents : he was not there. 'Tell him to come and see me,' she said to his father as she left the house.

On the third morning after her arrival Slimane appeared, and stood there in the doorway smiling. Once she had greeted him and made him sit down and have coffee with her, she plied him with questions about life in the village while she had been in Europe. Some of his friends had gone to become patriots, he said, and they were killing the French like flies. Her heart sank, but she said nothing. As she watched him smiling she was able to exult in the reflection that Slimane had been reachable, after all; she had proved that it was possible to make true friends of the younger people. But even while she was saying, 'How happy I am to see you, Slimane,' she remembered that their time together was now limited, and an expression of pain passed over her face as she finished the phrase. 'I shall not say a word to him about it,' she decided. If he, at least, still had the illusion of unbounded time lying ahead, he would somehow retain his aura of purity and innocence, and she would feel less anguish during the time they spent to-gether.

One day they went down the valley to see the caid, and discussed the long-planned trip to Abadla. Another day they started out at dawn to visit the tomb of Moulay Ali ben Said, where there was a spring of hot water. It was a tiny spot of oasis at the edge of a ridge of high dunes; per-haps fifty palms were there around the decayed shrine. In the shade of the rocks below the walls there was a ruined cistern into which the steaming water dribbled. They spread blankets on the sand nearby, at the foot of a small tamarisk, and took out their lunch. Before starting to eat, they drank handfuls of the water, which Slimane said was famed for its holiness. The palms rattled and hissed in the wind overhead.

'Allah has sent us the wind to make us cool while we eat,' Slimane said when he had finished his bread and dates.

'The wind has always been here,' she answered carelessly, 'and it always will be here.'

He sat up straight. 'No, no!' he cried. 'When Sidna Aissa has returned for forty days there will be no more Moslems and the world will end. Everything, the sky and the sun and the moon. And the wind too. Everything.' He looked at her with an expression of such satisfaction that she felt one of her occasional surges of anger against him.

'I see,' she said. 'Stand over by the spring a minute. I want to take your picture.' She had never understood why it was that the Moslems had conceded Jesus even this Pyrrhic victory, the coda to all creation : its inconsistency embarrassed her. Across the decayed tank she watched Slimane assume the traditional stiff attitude of a person about to be photographed, and an idea came into her head. For Christmas Eve, which would come within two weeks, she could make a crèche. She would invite Slimane to eat with her by the fireplace, and when midnight came she would take him in to see it.

She finished photographing Slimane; they gathered up the equipment and set out against the hot afternoon wind for the village. The sand sometimes swept by, stinging their faces with its invisible fringe. Fräulein Windling led the way this time, and they walked fast. The image of the crèche, illumined by candles, occurred to her several times on the way back over the rocky erg; it made her feel inexpressibly sad, for she could not help connecting it with the fact that everything was ending. They came to the point north of the village where the empty erg was cut across by the wander-

ing river valley. As they climbed slowly upward over the
fine sand, she found herself whispering : 'It's the right thing
to do.' '*Right* is not the word,' she thought, without being
able to find a better one. She was going to make a crèche
because she loved Christmas and wanted to share it with
Slimane. They reached the hotel shortly after sunset, and
she sent Slimane home in order to sit and plan her project
on paper.

It was only when she began actually to put the crèche together that she realized how much work it was going to be.
Early the next morning she asked Boufelja to find her an old
wooden crate. Before she had been busy even a half-hour,
she heard Slimane talking in the kitchen. Quickly she pushed
everything under the bed and went out onto the terrace.

'Slimane,' she said. 'I'm very busy. Come in the afternoon.' And that afternoon she told him that since she was
going to be working every morning until after the day of the
Christ Child, they would not be making any more long trips
during that time. He received the information glumly. 'I
know,' he said. 'You are getting ready for the holy day. I
understand.'

'When the holy day comes, we will have a feast,' she
assured him.

'If Allah wills.'

'I'm sorry,' she said, smiling.

He shrugged. 'Good-bye,' he told her.

Afternoons they still walked in the oasis or had tea on the
roof, but her mornings she spent in her room sewing, ham-
mering and sculpting. Once she had the platform con-
structed, she had to model the figures. She carried up a
great mass of wet clay from the river to her room. It was
two days before she managed to make a Virgin whose form
pleased her. From an old strip of muslin she fashioned a

convincing tent to house the Mother and the Child in its nest of tiny white chicken feathers. Shredded tamarisk needles made a fine carpet for the interior of the tent. Outside she poured sand, and then pushed the clay camels' long legs deep into it; one animal walked behind the other over the dune, and a Wise Man sat straight on top of each, his white *djellaba* falling in long pointed folds to either side of the camel's flanks. The Wise Men would come carrying sacks of almonds and very small liqueur chocolates wrapped in colored tinfoil. When she had the crèche finished, she put it on the floor in the middle of the room and piled tangerines and dates in front of it. With a row of candles burning behind it, and one candle on each side in front, it would look like a Moslem religious chromolithograph. She hoped the scene would be recognizable to Slimane; he might then be more easily persuaded of its poetic truth. She wanted only to suggest to him that the god with whom he was on such intimate terms was the god worshipped by the Nazarenes. It was not an idea she would ever try to express in words.

An additional surprise for the evening would be the new flash-bulb attachment to her camera, which Slimane had not yet seen. She intended to take a good many pictures of the crèche and of Slimane looking at it; these she would enlarge to show her pupils. She went and bought a new turban for Slimane; he had been wearing one for more than a year now. This was a man's turban, and very fine; ten meters of the softest Egyptian cotton.

The day before Christmas she overslept, duped by the heavy sky. Each winter the oasis had a few dark days; they were rare, but this was one of them. While she still lay there in bed, she heard the roar of the wind, and when she got up to look out of the window she found no world outside—

only a dim rose-gray fog that hid everything. The swirling sand sprayed ceaselessly against the glass; it had formed in long drifts on the floor of the terrace. When she went for breakfast, she wore her burnoose with the hood up around her face. The blast of the wind as she stepped out onto the terrace struck her with the impact of a solid object, and the sand gritted on the concrete floor under her shoes. In the dining-room Boufelja had bolted the shutters; he greeted her enthusiastically from the gloom inside, glad of her presence.

'A very bad day for your festival, alas, mademoiselle!' he observed as he set her coffee pot on the table.

'Tomorrow's the festival,' she said. 'It begins tonight.'

'I know. I know.' He was impatient with Nazarene feasts because the hours of their beginnings and ends were observed in so slipshod a manner. Moslem feasts began precisely, either at sundown or an hour before sunup, or when the new moon was first visible in the western sky at twilight. But the Nazarenes began their feasts whenever they felt like it.

She spent the morning in her room writing letters. By noon the air outside was darker with still more sand; the wind shook the hotel atop its rock as if it would hurl it over the tips of the palms below into the river-bed. Several times she rose and went to the window to stare out at the pink emptiness beyond the terrace. Storms made her happy, although she wished this one could have come after Christmas. She had imagined a pure desert night—cold, alive with stars, and the dogs yapping from the oasis. It might yet be that; there was still time, she thought, as she slipped her burnoose over her head to go in to lunch.

With the wind, the fireplace was an unsure blessing : besides the heat it gave, it provided the only light in the dining-room, but the smoke that belched from it burned her eyes and throat. The shutters at the windows rattled and pounded, covering the noise of the wind itself.

She got out of the dining-room as soon as she had finished eating, and hurried back to her room to sit through the slowly darkening afternoon, as she continued with her letter-writing and waited for the total extinction of daylight. Slimane was coming at eight. There would be enough time to carry everything into the dining-room before that, and to set the crèche up in the dark unused wing into which Boufelja was unlikely to go. But when she came to do it, she found that the wind's force was even greater than she had imagined. Again and again she made the trip between her room and the dining-room, carrying each object carefully wrapped in her burnoose. Each time she passed in front of the kitchen door she expected Boufelja to open it and discover her. She did not want him there when she showed the crèche to Slimane; he could see it tomorrow at breakfast.

Protected by the noise of the gale she succeeded in transporting all the parts to the far dark corner of the dining-room without alerting Boufelja. Long before dinner time the crèche was in readiness, awaiting only the lighting of the candles to be brought alive. She left a box of matches on the table beside it, and hurried back to her room to arrange her hair and change her clothing. The sand had sifted through her garments and was now everywhere; it showered from her underwear and stuck like sugar to her skin. Her watch showed a few minutes after eight when she went out.

Only one place had been laid at table. She waited, while the blinds chattered and banged, until Boufelja appeared carrying the soup tureen.

'What a bad night,' he said.

'You forgot to prepare for Slimane,' she told him. But he was not paying attention. 'He's stupid!' he exclaimed, beginning to ladle out the soup.

'Wait!' she cried. 'Slimane's coming. I mustn't eat until he comes.'

Still Boufelja misunderstood. 'He wanted to come into the dining-room,' he said. 'And he knows it's forbidden at dinner time.'

'But I invited him!' She looked at the lone soup plate on the table. 'Tell him to come in, and set another place.'

Boufelja was silent. He put the ladle back into the tureen. 'Where is he?' she demanded, and without waiting for him to reply she went on. 'Didn't I tell you he was going to have dinner with me tonight?' For suddenly she suspected that in her desire for secrecy she might indeed have neglected to mention the invitation to Boufelja.

'You didn't say anything,' he told her. 'I didn't know. I sent him home. But he'll back after dinner.'

'Oh, Boufelja!' she cried. 'You know Slimane never lies.'

He looked down at her with reproach on his face. 'I didn't know anything about mademoiselle's plans,' he said aggrievedly. This made her think for a swift instant that he had discovered the crèche, but she decided that if he had he would have spoken of it.

'Yes, yes, I know. I should have told you. It's my fault.'

'That's true, mademoiselle,' he said. And he served the remaining courses observing a dignified silence which she, still feeling some displeasure with him, did not urge him to break. Only at the end of the meal, when she had pushed back her chair from the table and sat studying the pattern of the flames in the fireplace, did he decide to speak. 'Mademoiselle will take coffee?'

'I do want some,' she said, trying to bring a note of enthusiasm into her voice. *'Bien,'* murmured Boufelja, and he left her alone in the room. When he returned carrying the coffee, Slimane was with him, and they were laughing, she noted, quite as though there had been no misunderstanding about dinner. Slimane stood by the door an instant, stamping his feet and shaking the sand from his burnoose. As he came forward to take her hand, she cried : 'Oh, Slimane, it's my fault! I forgot to tell Boufelja. It's terrible!'

'There is no fault, madame,' he said gravely. 'This is a festival.'

'Yes, this is a festival,' she echoed. 'And the wind's still blowing. Listen!'

Slimane would not take coffee, but Boufelja, ceding to her pressure, let her pour him out a cup, which he drank standing by the fireplace. She suspected him of being secretly pleased that Slimane had not managed to eat with her. When he had finished his coffee, he wished them good-night and went off to bed in his little room next to the kitchen.

They sat a while watching the fire, without talking. The wind rushed past in the emptiness outside, the blinds hammered. Fräulein Windling was content. Even if the first part of the celebration had gone wrong, the rest of the evening could still be pleasant.

She waited until she was sure that Boufelja had really gone to bed, and then she reached into her bag and brought out a small plastic sack full of chocolate creams, which she placed on the table.

'Eat,' she said carelessly, and she took a piece of candy herself. With some hesitation Slimane put out his hand to take the sack. When he had a chocolate in his mouth, she began to speak. She intended to tell him the story of the Nativity, a subject she already had touched upon many times during their excursions, but only in passing. This time

she felt she should tell him the entire tale. She expected
him to interrupt when he discovered that it was a religious
story, but he merely kept his noncommittal eyes on her and
chewed mechanically, showing that he followed her by
occasionally nodding his head. She became engrossed in
what she was saying, and began to use her arms in wide
gestures. Slimane reached for another chocolate and went
on listening.

She talked for an hour or more, aware as from a distance
of her own eloquence. When she told him about Bethlehem
she was really describing Slimane's own village, and the
house of Joseph and Mary was the house down in the *ksar*
where Slimane had been born. The night sky arched above
the Oued Zousfana and its stars glared down upon the cold
hammada. Across the erg on their camels came the Wise
Men in their burnooses and turbans, pausing at the crest
of the last great dune to look ahead at the valley where the
dark village lay. When she had finished, she blew her nose.

Slimane appeared to be in a state bordering on trance.
She glanced at him, expected him to speak, but as he did
not, she looked more closely at him. His eyes had an
obsessed, vacant expression, and although they were still
fixed on her face, she would have said that he was seeing
something much farther away than she. She sighed, not
wanting to make the decision to rouse him. The possibility
she would have liked to entertain, had she not been so conscious of its unlikelihood, was that the boy somehow had
been captivated by the poetic truth of the story, and was
reviewing it in his imagination. 'Certainly it could not be
the case,' she decided; it was more likely that he had ceased
some time back to listen to her words, and was merely
sitting there, only vaguely aware that she had come to the
end of her story.

Then he spoke. 'You're right. He was the King of Men.'

Fräulein Windling caught her breath and leaned forward, but he went on. 'And later Satan sent a snake with two heads. And Jesus killed it. Satan was angry with Him. He said : "Why did you kill my friend? Did it hurt you, perhaps?" And Jesus said : "I knew where it came from." And Satan put on a black burnoose. That's true,' he added, as he saw the expression of what he took to be simple disbelief on her face.

She sat up very straight and said : 'Slimane, what are you talking about? There are no such stories about Jesus. Nor about Sidna Aissa either.' She was not sure of the accuracy of this last statement; it was possible, she supposed, that such legends did exist among these people. 'You know those are just stories that have nothing to do with the truth.'

He did not hear her because he had already begun to talk. 'I'm not speaking of Sidna Aissa,' he said firmly. 'He was a Moslem prophet. I'm talking about Jesus, the prophet of the Nazarenes. Everyone knows that Satan sent Him a snake with two heads.'

She listened to the wind for an instant. 'Ah,' she said, and took another chocolate; she did not intend to carry the argument further. Soon she dug into her bag again and pulled out the turban, wrapped in red and white tissue paper.

'A present for you,' she said, holding it out to him. He seized it mechanically, placed it on his lap and remained staring down at it. 'Aren't you going to open it?' she demanded.

He nodded his head twice and tore open the paper. When he saw the pile of white cotton he smiled. Seeing his face at last come to life, she jumped up. 'Let's put it on you!' she exclaimed. He gave her one end, which she pulled taut by walking all the way to the door. Then with his hand holding the other end to his forehead, he turned slowly round and round, going toward her all the time, arranging the form of the turban as it wound itself about his head. 'Magnificent!' she cried. He went over to the row of black windows to look at himself.

'Can you see?' she asked.

'Yes, I can see the sides of it,' he told her. 'It's very beautiful.'

She walked back toward the center of the room. 'I'd like to take your picture, Slimane,' she said, seeing an immediate look of puzzlement appear in his face. 'Would you do me a favor? Go to my room and get the camera.'

'At night? You can take a picture at night?'

She nodded, smiling mysteriously. 'And bring me the yellow box on the bed.'

Keeping the turban on his head, he got into his burnoose, took her flashlight and went out, letting the wind slam the door. She hoped the sound had not wakened Boufelja; for an instant she listened while there was no sound but the roar of air rushing through the corridor outside. Then she ran to the dark wing of the room and struck a match. Quickly she lighted all the candles around the crèche, straightened a camel in the sand, and walked back around the corner to the fireplace. She would not have thought the candles could give so much light. The other end of the room was now brighter than the end where she stood. In a moment the door burst open and Slimane came back in, carrying the camera slung over his shoulder. He put it down carefully on the table. 'There was no yellow box on the bed,' he told her. Then his glance caught the further walls flickering with the unfamiliar light, and he began to walk toward the center of the room. She saw that this was the moment. 'Come,' she said, taking his arm and pulling him gently around the corner to where the crèche was finally visible, bright with its multiple shuddering points of light. Slimane said nothing; he stopped walking and stood completely still. After a moment of silence, she plucked tentatively at his arm. 'Come and see,' she urged him. They continued to walk toward the crèche; as they came up to it she had the impression that if she had not been there he would have reached out his hand and touched it, perhaps would have lifted the tiny gold-clad infant Jesus out of His bed of feathers. But he stood quietly, looking at it. Finally he said : 'You brought all that from Switzerland?'

'Of course not!' It was a little disappointing that he should not have recognized the presence of the desert in the picture, should not have sensed that the thing was of his place, and not an importation. 'I made it all here,' she said. She waited an instant. 'Do you like it?'

'Ah, yes,' he said with feeling. 'It's beautiful. I thought it came from Switzerland.'

To be certain that he understood the subject-matter, she began to identify the figures one by one, her voice taking on such an unaccustomed inflection of respect that he glanced up at her once in surprise. It was almost as if she too were seeing it for the first time. 'And the Wise Men are coming down out of the erg to see the child.'

'Why did you put all those almonds there?' asked Slimane, touching some with his forefinger.

'They're gifts for the little Jesus.'

'But what are you going to do with them?' he pursued.

'Eat them, probably, later,' she said shortly. 'Take one if you like. You say there was no yellow box on the bed?' She wanted to take the photographs while the candles were still of equal height.

'There was nothing but a sweater and some papers, madame.'

She left him there by the crèche, crossed the room and put on her burnoose. The darkness in the corridor was complete; there was no sign that Boufelja had awakened. She knew her room was in great disorder, and she played the beam of the flashlight around the floor before entering. In the welter of displaced things that strewed the little room there seemed small chance of finding anything. The feeble ray illumined one by one the meaningless forms made by the piling of disparate objects one on the other; the light moved over the floor, along the bed, behind the flimsy curtain of the armoire. Suddenly she stopped and turned the beam under the bed. The box was in front of her face; she had put it with the crèche.

'I mustn't fall,' she thought, running along the corridor. She forced herself to slow her pace to a walk, entered the dining room and shut the door after her carefully. Slimane was on his knees in the middle of the room, a small object of some sort in his hand. She noted with relief that he was amusing himself. 'I'm sorry it took me so long,' she exclaimed. 'I'd forgotten where I'd put it.' She was pulling her burnoose off over her head; now she hung it on a nail by the fireplace, and taking up the camera and the yellow box, she walked over to join him.

Perhaps a faint glimmer of guilt in his expression as he glanced up made her eyes stray along the floor toward another object lying nearby, similar to the one he held in his hand. It was one of the Wise Men, severed at the hips from his mount. The Wise Man in Slimane's hand was intact, but the camel had lost its head and most of its neck.

'Slimane! What are you doing?' she cried with undisguised anger. 'What have you done to the crèche?' She advanced around the corner and looked in its direction. There was not really much more than a row of candles and a pile of sand that had been strewn with tangerine peel and date stones; here and there a carefully folded square of lavender or pink tinfoil had been planted in the sand. All three of the Wise Men had been enlisted in Slimane's battle on the floor, the tent ravaged in the campaign to extricate the almonds piled inside, and the treasure sacks looted of their chocolate liqueurs. There was so sign anywhere of the infant Jesus or of his gold-lamé garment. She felt tears come into her eyes. Then she laughed shortly, and said : 'Well, it's finished. Yes?'

'Yes, madame,' he said calmly. 'Are you going to make the photograph now?' He got to his feet and laid the broken camel on the platform in the sand with the other debris.

Fräulein Windling spoke evenly. 'I wanted to take a picture of the crèche.'

He waited an instant, as if he were listening to a distant sound. Then he said : 'Should I put on my burnoose?'

'No.' She began to take out the flash-bulb attachment. When she had it ready, she took the picture before he had time to strike a pose. She saw his astonishment at the sudden bright light prolong itself into surprise that the thing was already done, and then become resentment at having been caught off his guard; but pretending to have seen nothing, she went on snapping covers shut. He watched her as she gathered up her things. 'Is it finished?' he said, disappointed. 'Yes,' she replied. 'It will be a very good picture.'

'Incha' Allah.'

She did not echo his piety. 'I hope you've enjoyed the festival,' she told him.

Slimane smiled widely. 'Ah yes, madame. Very much. Thank you.'

She let him out into the camel-square and turned the lock in the door. Quickly she went back into her room, wishing it were a clear night like other nights, when she could stand out on the terrace and look at the dunes and stars, or sit on the roof and hear the dogs, for in spite of the hour she was not sleepy. She cleared her bed of all the things that lay on top of it, and got in, certain that she was going to lie awake for a long time. For it had shaken her, the chaos Slimane had made in those few minutes of her absence. Across the seasons of their friendship she had come to think of him as being very nearly like herself, even though she knew he had not been that way when she first had met him. Now she saw the dangerous vanity at the core of that fantasy : she had assumed that somehow his association with her had automatically been for his ultimate good, that inevitably he had been undergoing a process of improvement as a result of knowing her. In her desire to see him change, she had begun to forget what Slimane was really like. 'I shall never understand him,' she thought helplessly, sure that just because she felt so close to him she would never be able to observe him dispassionately.

'This is the desert,' she told herself. 'Here food is not an adornment; it is meant to be eaten.' She had spread out food and he had eaten it. Any argument which attached blame to that could only be false. And so she lay there accusing herself. 'It has been too much head and high ideals,' she reflected, 'and not enough heart.' Finally she traveled on the sound of the wind into sleep.

At dawn when she awoke she saw that the day was going to be another dark one. The wind had dropped. She got up and shut the window. The early morning sky was heavy with cloud. She sank back into bed and fell asleep. It was later than usual when she rose, dressed, and went into the dining-room. Boufelja's face was strangely expressionless as he wished her good-morning. She supposed it was the memory of the last night's misunderstanding, still with him —or possibly he was annoyed at having had to clean up the remains of the crèche. Once she had sat down and spread her napkin across her lap, he unbent sufficiently to say to her : 'Happy festival.'

'Thank you. Tell me, Boufelja,' she went on, changing her inflection. 'When you brought Slimane back in after dinner last night, do you know where he had been? Did he tell you?

'He's a stupid boy,' said Boufelja. 'I told him to go home and eat and come back later. You think he did that? Never. He walked the whole time up and down in the courtyard here, outside the kitchen door, in the dark.'

'I understand!' exclaimed Fräulein Windling triumphantly. 'So he had no dinner at all.'

'I had nothing to give him,' he began, on the defensive.

'Of course not,' she said sternly. 'He should have gone home and eaten.'

'Ah, you see?' grinned Boufelja. 'That's what I told him to do.'

In her mind she watched the whole story being enacted : Slimane aloofly informing his father that he would be eating at the hotel with the Swiss lady, the old man doubtless making some scornful reference to her, and Slimane going out. Unthinkable, once he had been refused admittance to the dining-room, for him to go back and face the family's ridicule. 'Poor boy,' she murmured.

'The commandant wants to see you,' said Boufelja, making one of his abrupt conversational changes. She was surprised, since from one year to the next the captain never gave any sign of being aware of her existence; the hotel and the fort

were like two separate countries. 'Perhaps for the festival,'
Boufelja suggested, his face a mask. 'Perhaps,' she said uneasily.

When she had finished her breakfast, she walked across to
the gates of the fort. The sentry seemed to be expecting her.
One of the two young French soldiers was in the compound
painting a chair. He greeted her, saying that the captain
was in his office. She went up the long flight of stairs and
paused an instant at the top, looking down at the valley in
the unaccustomed gray light, noting how totally different it
looked from its usual self, on this dim day.

A voice from inside called out : *'Entrez, s'il vous plaît!'*
She opened the door and stepped in. The captain sat behind his desk; she had the unwelcome sensation of having
played this same scene on another occasion, in another
place. And she was suddenly convinced that she knew what
he was going to say. She seized the back of the empty chair
facing his desk. 'Sit down, Mademoiselle Windling,' he said,
rising halfway out of his seat, waving his arm, and sitting
again quickly.

There were several topographical maps on the wall behind him, marked with lavender and green chalk. The
captain looked at his desk and then at her, and said in a
clear voice : 'It is an unfortunate stroke of chance that I
should have to call you here on this holiday.' Fräulein
Windling sat down in the chair; leaning forward, she seemed
about to rest her elbows on his desk, but instead crossed her
legs and folded her arms tight. 'Yes?' she said, tense, waiting for the message. It came immediately, for which she was
conscious, even then, of being grateful to him. He told her
simply that the entire area had been closed to civilians; this
order applied to French nationals as well as to foreigners,
so she must not feel discriminated against. The last was said

with a wry attempt at a smile. 'This means that you will have to take tomorrow morning's truck,' he continued. 'The driver has already been advised of your journey. Perhaps another year, when the disturbances are over. . . .' ('Why does he say that?' she thought, 'when he knows it's the end, and the time of friendship is finished?') He rose and extended his hand.

She could not remember going out of the room and down the long stairway into the compound, but now she was standing outside the sentry gate beside the wall of the fort, with her hand on her forehead. 'Already,' she thought. 'It came so soon.' And it occurred to her that she was not going to be given the time to make amends to Slimane, so that it was really true she was never going to understand him. She walked up to the parapet to look down at the edge of the oasis for a moment, and then went back to her room to start packing. All day long she worked in her room, pulling out boxes, forcing herself to be aware only of the decisions she was making as to what was to be taken and what to be left behind once and for all.

At lunchtime Boufelja hovered near her chair. 'Ah, mademoiselle, how many years we have been together, and now it is finished!' 'Yes,' she thought, but there was nothing to do about it. His lamentations made her nervous and she was short with him. Then she felt guilt-stricken and said slowly, looking directly at him : 'I am very sad, Boufelja.' He sighed. 'Ay, mademoiselle, I know!'

By nightfall the pall of clouds had been blown away across the desert, and the western sky was partly clear. Fräulein Windling had finished all her packing. She went out onto the terrace, saw the dunes pink and glowing, and climbed the steps to the roof to look at the sunset. Great skeins of fiery storm-cloud streaked the sky. Mechanically she let her gaze follow the meanders of the river valley as it lost itself in the darkening *hammada* to the south. 'It is in the past,' she reminded herself; this was already the new era. The desert out there looked the same as it always had looked. But the sky, ragged, red and black, was like a handbill that had just been posted above it, announcing the arrival of war.

It was a betrayal, she was thinking, going back down the steep stairs, running her hand along the familiar rough mud wall to steady herself, and the French of course were the culprits. But beyond that she had the irrational and disagreeable conviction that the countryside itself had connived in the betrayal, that it was waiting to be transformed by the struggle. She went into her room and lit the small oil lamp; sitting down, she held her hands over it to warm them. At some point there had been a change : the people no longer wanted to go on living in the world they knew. The pressure of the past had become too great, and its shell had broken.

In the afternoon she had sent Boufelja to tell Slimane the news, and to ask him to be at the hotel at daybreak. During dinner she discussed only the details of departure and travel; when Boufelja tried to pull the talk in emotional directions, she did not reply. His commiseration was intolerable; she was not used to giving voice to her despair. When she got to her room she went directly to bed. The dogs barked half the night.

It was cold in the morning. Her hands ached as she gathered up the wet objects from around the washbowl on the table, and somehow she drove a sliver deep under the nail of her thumb. She picked some of it out with a needle, but the greater part remained. Before breakfast she stepped outside.

Standing in the waste-land between the hotel and the
fort, she looked down at the countryside's innocent face. The
padlocked gasoline pump, triumphant in fresh red and
orange paint, caught the pure early sunlight. For a moment
it seemed the only living thing in the landscape. She turned
around. Above the dark irregular mass of palm trees rose
the terraced village, calm under its morning veil of woodsmoke. She shut her eyes for an instant, and then went into
the hotel.

She could feel herself sitting stiffly in her chair while she
drank her coffee, and she knew she was being distant and
formal with Boufelja, but it was the only way she could be
certain of being able to keep going. Once he came to tell her
that Slimane had arrived bringing the donkey and its master
for her luggage. She thanked him and set down her coffee
cup. 'More?' said Boufelja. 'No,' she answered. 'Drink
another, mademoiselle,' he urged her. 'It's good on a cold
morning.' He poured it out and she drank part of it. There
was a knocking at the gate. One of the young soldiers had
been sent with a jeep to carry her out to the truck-stop on
the trail.

'I can't!' she cried, thinking of Slimane and the donkey.
The young soldier made it clear that he was not making an
offer, but giving an order. Slimane stood beside the donkey
outside the gate. While she began to speak with him the
soldier shouted : 'Does he want to come, the *gosse*? He can
come too, if he likes.' Slimane ran to get the luggage and
Fräulein Windling rushed inside to settle her bill. 'Don't
hurry,' the soldier called after her. 'There's plenty of time.'

Boufelja stood in the kitchen doorway. Now for the first
time it occurred to her to wonder what was going to become of him. With the hotel shut he would have no work.
When she had settled her account and given him a tip which

was much larger than she could afford, she took both his hands in hers and said : '*Mon cher* Boufelja, we shall see one another very soon.'

'Ah, yes,' he cried, trying to smile. 'Very soon, mademoiselle.'

She gave the donkey-driver some money, and got into the jeep beside the soldier. Slimane had finished bringing out the luggage and stood behind the jeep, kicking the tires. 'Have you got everything?' she called to him. 'Everything?' She would have liked to see for herself, but she was loath to go back into the room. Boufelja had disappeared; now he came hurrying out, breathless, carrying a pile of old magazines. 'It's all right,' she said. 'No, no! I don't want them.' The jeep was already moving ahead down the hill. In what seemed to her an unreasonably short time they had reached the boulders. When Fräulein Windling tried to lift out her briefcase the pain of the sliver under her nail made the tears start to her eyes, and she let go with a cry. Slimane glanced at her, surprised. 'I hurt my hand,' she explained. 'It's nothing.'

The bags had been piled in the shade. Sitting on a rock near the jeep, the soldier faced Fräulein Windling; from time to time he scanned the horizon behind her for a sign of the truck. Slimane examined the jeep from all sides; eventually he came to sit nearby. They did not say very much to one another. She was not sure whether it was because the soldier was with them, or because her thumb ached so constantly, but she sat quietly waiting, not wanting to talk.

It was a long time before the far-off motor made itself heard. When the truck was still no more than a puff of dust between sky and earth, the soldier was on his feet watching; an instant later Slimane jumped up. 'It is coming, madame,'

he said. Then he bent over, putting his face very close to
hers. 'I want to go with you to Colomb-Bechar,' he whispered. When she did not respond, because she was seeing
the whole story of their friendship unrolled before her, from
its end back to its beginning, he said louder, with great
urgency : 'Please, madame.'

Fräulein Windling hesitated only an instant. She raised
her head and looked carefully at the smooth brown face
that was so near. 'Of course, Slimane,' she said. It was clear
that he had not expected to hear this; his delight was in-
fectious, and she smiled as she watched him run to the pile
of bags and begin carrying them out into the sunlight to
align them in the dust beside the edge of the trail.

Later, when they were rattling along the *hammada*, she
in front beside the driver and Slimane squatting in the back
with a dozen men and a sheep, she considered her irrespon-
sible action in allowing him to make this absurd trip with
her all the way to Colomb-Bechar. Still, she knew she
wanted to give this ending to their story. A few times she
turned partially around in her seat to glance at him through
the dirty glass. He sat there in the smoke and dust, laughing like the others, with the hood of his burnoose hiding
most of his face.

It had been raining in Colomb-Bechar; the streets were
great puddles to reflect the clouded sky. At the garage they
found a surly Negro boy to help them carry the luggage to
the railway station. Her thumb hurt a little less.

'It's a cold town,' Slimane said to her as they went down
the main street. At the station they checked the bags and
then went outside to stand and watch a car being unloaded
from an open freight train : the roof of the automobile was
still white with snow from the high steppes. The day was
dark, and the wind rippled the surface of the water in the

flooded empty lots. Fräulein Windling's train would not be
leaving until late in the afternoon. They went to a restaurant
and ate a long lunch.

'You really will go back home tomorrow?' she asked him
anxiously at one point, while they were having fruit. 'You
know we have done a very wicked thing to your father and
mother. They will never forgive me.' A curtain seemed to
draw across Slimane's face. 'It doesn't matter,' he said
shortly.

After lunch they walked in the public garden and looked
at the eagles in their cages. A fine rain had begun to be
carried on the wind. The mud of the paths grew deeper.
They went back to the center of the town and sat down on
the terrace of a large, shabby modern café. The table at the
end was partly sheltered from the wet wind; they faced an
empty lot strewn with refuse. Nearby, spread out like the
bones of a camel fallen on the trail, were the rusted remains
of an ancient bus. A long, newly-felled date palm lay diagon-
ally across the greater part of the lot. Fräulein Windling
turned to look at the wet orange fiber of the stump, and
felt an idle pity for the tree. 'I'm going to have a Coca
Cola,' she declared. Slimane said he, too, would like one.

They sat there a long time. The fine rain slanted through
the air outside the arcades and hit the ground silently. She
had expected to be approached by beggars, but none arrived,
and now that the time had come to leave the café and go to
the station she was thankful to see that the day had passed
so easily. She opened her pocket-book, took out three thousand francs, and handed them to Slimane, saying : 'This will
be enough for everything. But you must buy your ticket
back home today. When you leave the railway station. Be
very careful of it.'

Slimane put the money inside his garments, rearranged

his burnoose, and thanked her. 'You understand, Slimane,' she said, detaining him with her hand, for he seemed about to rise from the table. 'I'm not giving you any money now, because I need what I have for my journey. But when I get to Switzerland I shall send you a little, now and then. Not much. A little.'

His face was swept by panic; she was perplexed.

'You haven't got my address,' he told her.

'No, but I shall send it to Boufelja's house,' she said, thinking that would satisfy him. He leaned toward her, his eyes intense. 'No, madame,' he said with finality. 'No. I have your address, and I shall send you mine. Then you will have it, and you can write to me.'

It did not seem worth arguing about. For most of the afternoon her thumb had not hurt too much; now, as the day waned, it had begun to ache again. She wanted to get up, find the waiter, and pay him. The fine rain still blew; the station was fairly far. But she saw that Slimane had something more to say. He leaned forward in his chair and looked down at the floor. 'Madame.' he began.

'Yes?' she said.

'When you are in your country and you think of me you will not be happy. It's true, no?'

'I shall be very sad,' she answered, rising.

Slimane got slowly to his feet and was quiet for an instant before going on. 'Sad because I ate the food out of the picture. That was very bad. Forgive me.'

The shrill sound of her own voice exclaiming. 'No!' startled her. 'No!' she cried. 'That was good!' She felt the muscles of her cheeks and lips twisting themselves into grimaces of weeping; fiercely she seized his arm and looked down into his face. *'Oh, mon pauvre petit!'* she sobbed, and then covered her face with both hands. She felt him gently touching her sleeve. A truck went by in the main street, shaking the floor.

With an effort she turned away and scratched in her bag for a handkerchief. 'Come,' she said, clearing her throat. 'Call the waiter.'

They arrived at the station cold and wet. The train was being assembled; passengers were not allowed to go out onto the platform and were sitting on the floor inside. While Fräulein Windling bought her ticket Slimane went to get the bags from the checkroom. He was gone for a long time. When he arrived he came with his burnoose thrown back over his shoulders, grinning triumphantly, with three valises piled on his head. A man in ragged European jacket and trousers followed behind carrying the rest. As he came nearer she saw that the man held a slip of paper between his teeth.

The ancient compartment smelled of varnish. Through the window she could see, above some remote western reach of waste-land, a few strips of watery white sky. Slimane wanted to cover the seats with the luggage, so that no one would come into the compartment. 'No,' she said. 'Put them in the racks.' There were very few passengers in the coach. When everything was in place, the porter stood outside in the corridor and she noticed that he still held the slip of paper between his teeth. He counted the coins she gave him and pocketed them. Then quickly he handed the paper to Slimane, and was gone.

Fräulein Windling bent down a bit, to try and see her face in the narrow mirror that ran along the back of the seat. There was not enough light; the oil lantern above illumined only the ceiling, its base casting a leaden shadow over everything beneath. Suddenly the train jolted and made a series of crashing sounds. She took Slimane's head between her hands and kissed the middle of his forehead. 'Please get down from the train,' she told him. 'We can talk here.' She pointed to the window and began to pull on the torn leather strap that lowered it.

Slimane looked small on the dark platform, staring up at her as she leaned out. Then the train started to move. She thought surely it would go only a few feet and then stop, but it continued ahead, slowly. Slimane walked with it, keeping abreast of her window. In his hand was the paper the porter had given him. He held it up to her, crying : 'Here is my address! Send it here!'

She took it, and kept waving as the train went faster, kept calling : 'Good-bye!' He continued to walk quickly along beside the window, increasing his gait until he was running, until all at once there was no more platform. She leaned far out, looking backward, waving; straightway he was lost in the darkness and rain. A bonfire blazed orange by the track, and the smoke stung in her nostrils. She pulled up the window, glanced at the slip of paper she had in her hand, and sat down. The train jolted her this way and that; she went on staring at the paper, although now it was in shadow; and she remembered the first day, long ago, when the child Slimane had stood outside the door watching her, stepping back out of her range of vision each time she turned to look at him. The words hastily printed for him on the scrap of paper by the porter were indeed an address, but the address was in Colomb-Bechar. 'They said he tried to run away. But he didn't get very far.' Each detail of his behavior as she went back over it clarified the pattern for her. 'He's too young to be a soldier,' she told herself. 'They won't take him.' But she knew they would.

Her thumb was hot and swollen; sometimes it seemed almost that its throbbing accompanied the side-to-side jolting of the coach. She looked out at the few remaining patches of colorless light in the sky. Sooner or later, she argued, he would have done it.

'Another year, perhaps,' the captain had said. She saw her own crooked, despairing smile in the dark window-glass beside her face. Maybe Slimane would be among the fortunate ones, an early casualty. 'If only death were absolutely certain in wartime,' she thought wryly, 'the waiting would not be so painful.' Listing and groaning, the train began its long climb upwards over the plateau.

The Hyena

A stork was passing over desert country on his way north. He was thirsty, and he began to look for water. When he came to the mountains of Khang el Ghar, he saw a pool at the bottom of a ravine. He flew down between the rocks and lighted at the edge of the water. Then he walked in and drank.

At that moment a hyena limped up and, seeing the stork standing in the water, said : 'Have you come a long way?' The stork had never seen a hyena before. 'So this is what a hyena is like,' he thought. And he stood looking at the hyena because he had been told that if the hyena can put a little of his urine on someone, that one will have to walk after the hyena to whatever place the hyena wants him to go.

'It will be summer soon,' said the stork. 'I am on my way north.' At the same time, he walked further out into the pool, so as not to be so near the hyena. The water here was deeper, and he almost lost his balance and had to flap his wings to keep upright. The hyena walked to the other side of the pool and looked at him from there.

'I know what is in your head,' said the hyena. 'You believe the story about me. You think I have that power? Perhaps long ago hyenas were like that. But now they are the same as everyone else. I could wet you from here with my urine if I wanted to. But what for? If you want to be unfriendly, go to the middle of the pool and stay there.'

The stork looked around at the pool and saw that there was no spot in it where he could stand and be out of reach of the hyena.

'I have finished drinking,' said the stork. He spread his wings and flapped out of the pool. At the edge he ran quickly ahead and rose into the air. He circled above the pool, looking down at the hyena.

'So you are the one they call the ogre,' he said. 'The world is full of strange things.'

The hyena looked up. His eyes were narrow and crooked. 'Allah brought us all here,' he said. 'You know that. You are the one who knows about Allah.'

The stork flew a little lower. 'That is true,' he said. 'But I am surprised to hear you say it. You have a very bad name, as you yourself just said. Magic is against the will of Allah.'

The hyena tilted his head. 'So you still believe the lies!' he cried.

'I have not seen the inside of your bladder,' said the stork. 'But why does everyone say you can make magic with it?'

'Why did Allah give you a head, I wonder? You have not learned how to use it.' But the hyena spoke in so low a voice that the stork could not hear him.

'Your words got lost,' said the stork, and he let himself drop lower.

The hyena looked up again. 'I said : "Don't come too near me. I might lift my leg and cover you with magic !" ' He laughed, and the stork was near enough to see that his teeth were brown.

'Still, there must be some reason,' the stork began. Then he looked for a rock high above the hyena, and settled himself on it. The hyena sat and stared up at him. 'Why does everyone hate you?' the stork went on. 'Why do they call you an ogre? What have you done?'

The hyena squinted. 'You are very lucky,' he told the stork. 'Men never try to kill you, because they think you are holy. They call you a saint and a sage. And yet you seem like neither a saint nor a sage.'

'What do you mean?' said the stork quickly.

'If you really understood, you would know that magic is a grain of dust in the wind, and that Allah has power over everything. You would not be afraid.'

The stork stood for a long time, thinking. He lifted one leg and held it bent in front of him. The ravine grew red as the sun went lower. And the hyena sat quietly looking up at the stork, waiting for him to speak.

Finally the stork put his leg down, opened his bill, and said: 'You mean that if there is no magic, the one who sins is the one who believes there is.'

The hyena laughed. 'I said nothing about sin. But you did, and you are the sage. I am not in the world to tell anyone what is right or wrong. Living from night to night is enough. Everyone hopes to see me dead.'

The stork lifted his leg again and stood thinking. The last daylight rose into the sky and was gone. The cliffs at the sides of the ravine were lost in the darkness.

At length the stork said: 'You have given me something to think about. That is good. But now night has come. I must go on my way.' He raised his wings and started to fly straight out from the boulder where he had stood. The hyena listened. He heard the stork's wings beating the air slowly, and then he heard the sound of the stork's body as it hit the cliff on the other side of the ravine. He climbed up over the rocks and found the stork. 'Your wing is broken,' he said. 'It would have been better for you to go while there was still daylight.'

'Yes,' said the stork. He was unhappy and afraid.

'Come home with me,' the hyena told him. 'Can you walk?'

'Yes,' said the stork. Together they made their way down the valley. Soon they came to a cave in the side of the mountain. The hyena went in first and called out: 'Bend your head.' When they were well inside, he said: 'Now you can put your head up. The cave is high here.'

There was only darkness inside. The stork stood still. 'Where are you?' he said.

'I am here,' the hyena answered, and he laughed.

'Why are you laughing?' asked the stork.

'I was thinking that the world is strange,' the hyena told him. 'The saint has come into my cave because he believed in magic.'

'I don't understand,' said the stork.

'You are confused. But at least now you can believe that I have no magic. I am like anyone else in the world.'

The stork did not answer right away. He smelled the stench of the hyena very near him. Then he said, with a sigh: 'You are right, of course. There is no power beyond the power of Allah.'

'I am happy,' said the hyena, breathing into his face. 'At last you understand.' Quickly he seized the stork's neck and tore it open. The stork flapped and fell on his side.

'Allah gave me something better than magic,' the hyena said under his breath. 'He gave me a brain.'

The stork lay still. He tried to say once more: 'There is no power beyond the power of Allah.' But his bill merely opened very wide in the dark.

The hyena turned away. 'You will be dead in a minute,'

he said over his shoulder. 'In ten days I shall come back. By then you will be ready.'

Ten days later the hyena went to the cave and found the stork where he had left him. The ants had not been there. 'Good,' he said. He devoured what he wanted and went outside to a large flat rock above the entrance to the cave. There in the moonlight he stood a while, vomiting.

He ate some of his vomit and rolled for a long time in the rest of it, rubbing it deep into his coat. Then he thanked Allah for eyes that could see the valley in the moonlight, and for a nose that could smell the carrion on the wind. He rolled some more and licked the rock under him. For a while he lay there panting. Soon he got up and limped on his way.

He of the Assembly

He salutes all parts of the sky and the earth where it is bright. He thinks the color of the amethysts of Aguelmous will be dark if it has rained in the valley of Zerekten. 'The eye wants to sleep,' he says, 'but the head is no mattress.' When it rained for three days and water covered the flatlands outside the ramparts, he slept by the bamboo fence at the Café of the Two Bridges.

It seems there was a man named Ben Tajah who went to Fez to visit his cousin. The day he came back he was walking in the Djemaa el Fna, and he saw a letter lying on the pavement. He picked it up and found that his name was written on the envelope. He went to the Café of the Two Bridges with the letter in his hand, sat down on a mat and opened the envelope. Inside was a paper which read : 'The sky trembles and the earth is afraid, and the two eyes are not brothers.' Ben Tajah did not understand, and he was very unhappy because his name was on the envelope. It made him think that Satan was nearby. He of the Assembly was sitting in the same part of the café. He was listening to the wind in the telephone wires. The sky was almost empty of daytime light. 'The eye wants to sleep,' he thought, 'but the head is no mattress. I know what that is, but I have forgotten it.' Three days is a long time for rain to keep falling on flat bare ground. 'If I got up and ran down the street,' he thought, 'a policeman would follow me and call to me to stop. I would run faster, and he would run after me. When he shot at me. I'd duck around the corners of houses.' He felt the rough dried mud of the wall under his fingertips. 'And I'd be running through the streets looking for a place to hide, but no door would be open, until finally I came to one door that was open, and I'd go in through the rooms and courtyards until finally I came to the kitchen. The old woman would be there.' He stopped and wondered for a moment why an old woman should be there alone in the kitchen at that hour. She was stirring a big kettle of soup on the stove. 'And I'd look for a place to hide there in the kitchen, and there'd be no place. And I'd be waiting to hear the policeman's footsteps, because he wouldn't miss the open door. And I'd look in the dark corner of the room where she kept the charcoal, but it wouldn't be dark enough. And the old woman would turn and look at me and say : "If you're trying to get away, my boy, I can help you. Jump into the soup-kettle." ' The wind sighed in the telephone wires. Men came into the Café of the Two Bridges with their garments flapping. Ben Tajah sat on his mat. He had put the letter away, but first he had stared at it a long time. He of the Assembly leaned back and looked at the sky. 'The old woman,' he said to himself. 'What is she trying to do? The soup is hot. It may be a trap. I may find there's no way out, once I get down there.' He wanted a pipe of kif, but he was afraid the policeman would run into the kitchen before he was able to smoke it. He said to the old woman : 'How can I get in? Tell me.' And it seemed to him that he heard footsteps in the street, or perhaps even in one of the rooms of the house. He leaned over the stove and looked down into the kettle. It was dark and very hot down in there. Steam was coming up in clouds, and there was a thick smell in the air that made it hard to breathe. 'Quick!' said the old woman, and she un-

rolled a rope ladder and hung it over the edge of the kettle.
He began to climb down, and she leaned over and looked
after him. 'Until the other world!' he shouted. And he
climbed all the way down. There was a rowboat below.
When he was in it he tugged on the ladder and the old
woman began to pull it up. And at that instant the policeman ran in, and two more were with him, and the old
woman had just the time to throw the ladder down into the
soup. 'Now they are going to take her to the commissariat,'
he thought, 'and the poor woman only did me a favor.' He
rowed around in the dark for a few minutes, and it was
very hot. Soon he took off his clothes. For a while he could
see the round top of the kettle up above, like a porthole in
the side of a ship, with the heads of the policemen looking
down in, but then it grew smaller as he rowed, until it was
only a light. Sometimes he could find it and sometimes he
lost it, and finally it was gone. He was worried about the
old woman, and he thought he must find a way to help her.
No policeman can go into the Café of the Two Bridges because it belongs to the Sultan's sister. This is why there is
so much kif smoke inside that a *berrada* can't fall over even
if it is pushed, and why most customers like to sit outside,
and even there keep one hand on their money. As long as
the thieves stay inside and their friends bring them food and
kif, they are all right. One day police headquarters will
forget to send a man to watch the café, or one man will
leave five minutes before the other gets there to take his
place. Outside everyone smokes kif too, but only for an hour
or two—not all day and night like the ones inside. He of the
Assembly had forgotten to light his *sebsi*. He was in a café
where no policeman could come, and he wanted to go away
to a kif world where the police were chasing him. 'This is
the way we are now,' he thought. 'We work backwards.' If

we have something good, we look for something bad instead.' He lighted the *sebsi* and smoked it. Then he blew the hard ash out of the *chqaf*. It landed in the brook beside the second bridge. 'The world is too good. We can only work forward if we make it bad again first.' This made him sad, so he stopped thinking, and filled his *sebsi*. While he was smoking it, Ben Tajah looked in his direction, and although they were facing each other, He of the Assembly did not notice Ben Tajah until he got up and paid for his tea. Then he looked at him because he took such a long time getting up off the floor. He saw his face and he thought : 'That man has no one in the world.' The idea made him feel cold. He filled his *sebsi* again and lighted it. He saw the man as he was going to go out of the café and walk alone down the long road outside the ramparts. In a little while he himself would have to go out to the *souks* to try and borrow money for dinner. When he smoked a lot of kif he did not like his aunt to see him, and he did not want to see her. 'Soup and bread. No one can want more than that. Will thirty francs be enough the fourth time? The *qahouaji* wasn't satisfied last night. But he took it. And he went away and let me sleep. A Moslem, even in the city, can't refuse his brother shelter.' He was not convinced, because he had been born in the mountains, and so he kept thinking back and forth in this way. He smoked many *chqofa*, and when he got up to go out into the street he found that the world had changed.

Ben Tajah was not a rich man. He lived alone in a room near Bab Doukkala, and he had a stall in the bazaars where he sold coathangers and chests. Often he did not open the shop because he was in bed with a liver attack. At such times he pounded on the floor from his bed, using a brass pestle, and the postman who lived downstairs brought him up some food. Sometimes he stayed in bed for a week at a time. Each morning and night the postman came in with a tray. The food was not very good because the postman's wife did not understand much about cooking. But he was glad to have it. Twice he had brought the postman a new chest to keep clothes and blankets in. One of the postman's wives a few years before had taken a chest with her when she had left him and gone back to her family in Kasba Tadla. Ben Tajah himself had tried having a wife for a while because he needed someone to get him regular meals and to wash his clothes, but the girl was from the mountains, and was wild. No matter how much he beat her she would not be tamed. Everything in the room got broken, and finally he had to put her out into the street. 'No more women will get into my house,' he told his friends in the bazaars, and they laughed. He took home many women, and one day he found that he had *en noua*. He knew that was a bad disease, because it stays in the blood and eats the nose from inside. 'A man loses his nose only long after he has already lost his head.' He asked a doctor for medicine. The doctor gave him a paper and told him to take it to the Pharmacie de l'Etoile. There he bought six vials of penicillin in a box. He took them home and tied each little bottle with a silk thread, stringing them so that they made a necklace. He wore this always around his neck, taking care that the glass vials touched his skin. He thought it likely that by now he was cured, but his cousin in Fez had just told him that he must go on wearing the medicine for another three months, or at least until the beginning of the moon of Chouwal. He had thought about this now and then on the way home, sitting in the bus for two days, and he had decided that his cousin was too cautious. He stood in the

Djemaa el Fna a minute watching the trained monkeys, but the crowd pushed too much, so he walked on. When he got home he shut the door and put his hand in his pocket to pull out the envelope, because he wanted to look at it again inside his own room, and be sure that the name written on it was beyond a doubt his. But the letter was gone. He remembered the jostling in the Djemaa el Fna. Someone had reached into his pocket and imagined his hand was feeling money, and taken it. Yet Ben Tajah did not truly believe this. He was convinced that he would have known such a theft was happening. There had been a letter in his pocket. He was not even sure of that. He sat down on the cushions. 'Two days in the bus,' he thought. 'Probably I'm tired. I found no letter.' He searched in his pocket again, and it seemed to him he could still remember how the fold of the envelope had felt. 'Why would it have my name on it? I never found any letter at all.' Then he wondered if anyone had seen him in the café with the envelope in one hand and the sheet of paper in the other, looking at them both for such a long time. He stood up. He wanted to go back to the Café of the Two Bridges and ask the *qahouaji*: 'Did you see me an hour ago? Was I looking at a letter?' If the *qahouaji* said, 'Yes,' then the letter was real. He repeated the words aloud : 'The sky trembles and the earth is afraid, and the two eyes are not brothers.' In the silence afterwards the memory of the sound of the words frightened him. 'If there was no letter, where are these words from?' And he shivered because the answer to that was : 'From Satan.' He was about to open the door when a new fear stopped him. The *qahouaji* might say, 'No,' and this would be still worse, because it would mean that the words had been put directly into his head by Satan, that Satan had chosen him to reveal Himself to. In that case He might

appear at any moment. '*Ach haddou laillaha ill'Allah. . . ,*'
he prayed, holding his two forefingers up, one on each
side of him. He sat down again and did not move. In the
street the children were crying. He did not want to hear the
qahouaji say : 'No. You had no letter.' If he knew that
Satan was coming to tempt him, he would have that much
less power to keep Him away with his prayers, because he
would be more afraid.

He of the Assembly stood. Behind him was a wall. In his
hand was the *sebsi*. Over his head was the sky, which he felt
was about to burst into light. He was leaning back looking
at it. It was dark on the earth, but there was still light up
there behind the stars. Ahead of him was the *pissoir* of the
Carpenters' Souk which the French had put there. People
said only Jews used it. It was made of tin, and there was a
puddle in front of it that reflected the sky and the top of
the *pissoir*. It looked like a boat in the water. Or like a pier
where boats land. Without moving from where he stood,
He of the Assembly saw it approaching slowly. He was going
toward it. And he remembered he was naked, and put his
hand over his sex. In a minute the rowboat would be bump-
ing against the pier. He steadied himself on his legs and
waited. But at that moment a large cat ran out of the
shadow of the wall and stopped in the middle of the street
to turn and look at him with an evil face. He saw its two
eyes and for a while could not take his own eyes away. Then
the cat ran across the street and was gone. He was not sure
what had happened, and he stood very still looking at the
ground. He looked back at the *pissoir* reflected in the puddle
and thought : 'It was a cat on the shore, nothing else.' But
the cat's eyes had frightened him. Instead of being like
cats' eyes, they had looked like the eyes of a person who was
interested in him. He made himself forget he had had this

thought. He was still waiting for the rowboat to touch the landing pier, but nothing had happened. It was going to stay where it was, that near the shore but not near enough to touch. He stood still a long time, waiting for something to happen. Then he began to walk very fast down the street toward the bazaars. He had just remembered that the old woman was in the police station. He wanted to help her, but first he had to find out where they had taken her. 'I'll have to go to every police station in the Medina,' he thought, and he was not hungry any more. It was one thing to promise himself he would help her when he was far from land, and another when he was a few doors from a commissariat. He walked by the entrance. Two policemen stood in the doorway. He kept walking. The street curved and he was alone. 'This night is going to be a jewel in my crown,' he said, and he turned quickly to the left and went along a dark passageway. At the end he saw flames, and he knew that Mustapha would be there tending the fire of the bakery. He crawled into the mud hut where the oven was. 'Ah, the jackal has come back from the forest!' said Mustapha. He of the Assembly shook his head. 'This is a bad world,' he told Mustapha. 'I've got no money,' Mustapha said. He of the Assembly did not understand. 'Everything goes backwards,' he said. 'It's bad now, and we have to make it still worse if we want to go forwards.' Mustapha saw that He of the Assembly was *mkiyif ma rassou* and was not interested in money. He looked at him in a more friendly way and said : 'Secrets are not between friends. Talk.' He of the Assembly told him that an old woman had done him a great favor, and because of that three policemen had arrested her and taken her to the police station. 'You must go for me to the commissariat and ask them if they have an old woman there.' He pulled out his *sebsi* and took a very long time filling it.

When he finished it he smoked it himself and did not offer any to Mustapha, because Mustapha never offered him any of his. 'You see how full of kif my head is,' he said laughing. 'I can't go.' Mustapha laughed too and said it would not be a good idea, and that he would go for him.

'I was there, and I heard him going away for a long time, so long that he had to be gone, and yet he was still there, and his footsteps were still going away. He went away and there was nobody. There was the fire and I moved away from it. I wanted to hear a sound like a muezzin crying *Allah akbar!* or a French plane from the Pilot Base flying over the Medina, or news on the radio. It wasn't there. And when the wind came in the door it was made of dust high as a man. A night to be chased by dogs in the Mellah. I looked in the fire and I saw an eye in there, like the eye that's left when you burn *chibb* and you know there was a *djinn* in the house. I got up and stood. The fire was making a noise like a voice. I think it was talking. I went out and walked along the street. I walked a long time and I came to Bab el Khemiss. It was dark there and the wind was cold. I went to the wall where the camels were lying and stood there. Sometimes the men have fires and play songs on their *aouadas*. But they were asleep. All snoring. I walked again and went to the gate and looked out. The big trucks went by full of vegetables and I thought I would like to be on a truck and ride all night. Then in another city I would be a soldier and go to Algeria. Everything would be good if we had a war. I thought a long time. Then I was so cold I turned around and walked again. It was as cold as the belly of the oldest goat of Ijoukak. I thought I heard a muezzin and I stopped and listened. The only thing I heard was the water running in the *seguia* that carries the water out to the gardens. It was near the *mçid* of Moulay Boujemaa.

I heard the water running by and I felt cold. Then I knew I was cold because I was afraid. In my head I was thinking : "If something should happen that never happened before, what would I do?" You want to laugh? Hashish in your heart and wind in your head. You think it's like your grandmother's prayer-mat. This is the truth. This isn't a dream brought back from another world past the customs like a teapot from Mecca. I heard the water and I was afraid. There were some trees by the path ahead of me. You know at night sometimes it's good to pull out the *sebsi* and smoke. I smoked and I started to walk. And then I heard something. Not a muezzin. Something that sounded like my name. But it came up from below, from the *seguia, Allah istir!* And I walked with my head down. I heard it again saying my name, a voice like water, like the wind moving the leaves in the trees, a woman. It was a woman calling me. The wind was in the trees and the water was running, but there was a woman too. You think it's kif. No, she was calling my name. Now and then, not very loud. When I was under the trees it was louder, and I heard that the voice was my mother's. I heard that the way I can hear you. Then I knew the cat was not a cat, and I knew that Aïcha Qandicha wanted me. I thought of other nights when perhaps she had been watching me from the eyes of a cat or a donkey. I knew she was not going to catch me. Nothing in the seven skies could make me turn around. But I was cold and afraid and when I licked my lips my tongue had no spit on it. I was under the *safsaf* trees and I thought : "She's going to reach down and try to touch me. But she can't touch me from the front and I won't turn around, not even if I hear a pistol." I remembered how the policeman had fired at me and how I'd found only one door open. I began to yell : "You threw me the ladder and told me to climb down! You brought me here! The filthiest whore in the Mellah, with the pus coming out of her, is a thousand times cleaner than you, daughter of all the padronas and dogs in seven worlds." I got past the trees and I began to run. I called up to the sky so she could hear my voice behind : "I hope the police put a hose in your mouth and pump you full of salt water until you crack open!" I thought : "To-morrow I'm going to buy *fasoukh* and *tib* and *nidd* and *hasalouba* and *mska* and all the *bakhour* in the Djemaa, and put them in the *mijmah* and burn them, and walk back and forth over the *mijmah* ten times slowly, so the smoke can clean out all my clothes. Then I'll see if there's an eye in the ashes afterwards. If there is, I'll do it all over again right away. And every Thursday I'll buy the *bakhour* and every Friday I'll burn it. That will be strong enough to keep her away." If I could find a window and look through and see what they're doing to the old woman! If only they could kill her! I kept running. There were a few people in the streets. I didn't look to see where I was going, but I went to the street near Mustapha's oven where the commissariat was. I stopped running before I got to the door. The one standing there saw me before that. He stepped out and raised his arm. He said to me : "Come here." '

He of the Assembly ran. He felt as though he were on horseback. He did not feel his legs moving. He saw the road coming toward him and the doors going by. The policeman had not shot at him yet, but it was worse than the other time because he was very close behind and he was blowing his whistle. 'The policeman is old. At least thirty-five. I can run faster.' But from any street others could come. It was dangerous and he did not want to think about danger. He of the Assembly let songs come into his head. When it rains in the valley of Zerekten the amethysts are darker in Aguel-

mous. The eye wants to sleep but the head is no mattress.
It was a song. Ah, my brother, the ink on the paper is like
smoke in the air. What words are there to tell how long a
night can be? Drunk with love, I wander in the dark. He
was running through the dye-souk, and he splashed into a
puddle. The whistle blew again behind him, like a crazy
bird screaming. The sound made him feel like laughing, but
that did not mean he was not afraid. He thought : 'If I'm
seventeen I can run faster. That has to be true.' It was very
dark ahead. He had to slow his running. There was no time
for his eyes to get used to the dark. He nearly ran into the
wall of the shop at the end of the street. He turned to the
right and saw the narrow alley ahead of him. The police
had tied the old woman naked to a table with her thin legs
wide apart and were sliding electrodes up inside her. He
ran ahead. He could see the course of the alley now even
in the dark. Then he stopped dead, moved to the wall, and
stood still. He heard the footsteps slowing down. 'He's going
to turn to the left.' And he whispered aloud : 'It ends that
way.' The footsteps stopped and there was silence. The
policeman was looking into the silence and listening into the
dark to the left and to the right. He of the Assembly could
not see him or hear him, but he knew that was what he was
doing. He did not move. When it rains in the valley of
Zerekten. A hand seized his shoulder. He opened his mouth
and swiftly turned, but the man had moved and was push-
ing him from the side. He felt the wool of the man's *djellaba*
against the back of his hand. He had gone through a door
and the man had shut it without making any noise. Now
they both stood still in the dark, listening to the policeman
walking quickly by outside the door. Then the man struck
a match. He was facing the other way, and there was a
flight of stairs ahead. The man did not turn around, but he

said, 'Come up,' and they both climbed the stairs. At the
top the man took out a key and opened a door. He of the
Assembly stood in the doorway while the man lit a candle.
He liked the room because it had many mattresses and
cushions and a white sheepskin under the tea-tray in the
corner on the floor. The man turned around and said : 'Sit
down.' His face looked serious and kind and unhappy. He
of the Assembly had never seen it before, but he knew it
was not the face of a policeman. He of the Assembly pulled
out his *sebsi*.

Ben Tajah looked at the boy and asked him : 'What did
you mean when you said down there : "It ends that way?"
I heard you say it.' The boy was embarrassed. He smiled
and looked at the floor. Ben Tajah felt happy to have him
there. He had been standing outside the door downstairs in
the dark for a long time, trying to make himself go to the
Café of the Two Bridges and talk to the *qahouaji*. In his
mind it was almost as though he already had been there and
spoken with him. He had heard the *qahouaji* telling him
that he had seen no letter, and he had felt his own dismay.
He had not wanted to believe that, but he would be willing
to say yes, I made a mistake and there was no letter, if only
he could find out where the words had come from. For the
words were certainly in his head : '. . . and the two eyes are
not brothers.' That was like the footprint found in the
garden the morning after a bad dream, the proof that there
had been a reason for the dream, that something had been
there after all. Ben Tajah had not been able to go or to stay.
He had started and stopped so many times that now,
although he did not know it, he was very tired. When a
man is tired he mistakes the hopes of children for the know-
ledge of men. It seemed to him that He of the Assembly's
words had a meaning all for him. Even though the boy

might not know it, he could have been sent by Allah to
help him at that minute. In a nearby street a police whistle
blew. The boy looked at him. Ben Tajah did not care very
much what the answer would be, but he said : 'Why are
they looking for you?' The boy held out his lighted *sebsi*
and his *mottoui* fat with kif. He did not want to talk because he was listening. Ben Tajah smoked kif only when a
friend offered it to him, but he understood that the police
had begun once more to try to enforce their law against
kif. Each year they arrested people for a few weeks, and
then stopped arresting them. He looked at the boy, and
decided that probably he smoked too much. With the *sebsi*
in his hand he was sitting very still listening to the voices
of some passers-by in the street below. 'I know who he is,'
one said. 'I've got his name from Mustapha.' 'The baker?'
'That's the one.' They walked on. The boy's expression was
so intense that Ben Tajah said to him : 'It's nobody. Just
people.' He was feeling happy because he was certain that
Satan would not appear before him as long as the boy was
with him. He said quietly : 'Still you haven't told me why
you said : "It ends that way." ' The boy filled his *sebsi*
slowly and smoked all the kif in it. 'I meant,' he said,
'thanks to Allah. Praise the sky and the earth where it is
bright. What else can you mean when something ends?'
Ben Tajah nodded his head. Pious thoughts can be of as
much use for keeping Satan at a distance as camphor or
bakhour dropped onto hot coals. Each holy word is worth
a high column of smoke, and the eyelids do not smart afterward. 'He has a good heart,' thought Ben Tajah, 'even
though he is probably a guide for the Nazarenes.' And he
asked himself why it would not be possible for the boy to
have been sent to protect him from Satan. 'Probably not.
But it could be.' The boy offered him the *sebsi*. He took it

and smoked it. After that Ben Tajah began to think that he would like to go to the Café of the Two Bridges and speak to the *qahouaji* about the letter. He felt that if the boy went with him the *qahouaji* might say there had been a letter, and that even if the man could not remember, he would not mind so much because he would be less afraid. He waited until he thought the boy was not nervous about going into the street, and then he said : 'Let's go out and get some tea.' 'Good,' said the boy. He was not afraid of the police if he was with Ben Tajah. They went through the empty streets, crossed the Djemaa el Fna and the garden beyond. When they were near the café, Ben Tajah said to the boy : 'Do you know the Café of the Two Bridges?' The boy said he always sat there, and Ben Tajah was not surprised. It seemed to him that perhaps he had even seen him there. He seized the boy's arm. 'Were you there today?' he asked him. The boy said, 'Yes,' and turned to look at him. He let go of the arm. 'Nothing,' he said. 'Did you ever see me there?' They came to the gate of the café and Ben Tajah stopped walking. 'No,' the boy said. They went across the first bridge and then the second bridge, and sat down in a corner. Not many people were left outside. Those inside were making a great noise. The *qahouaji* brought the tea and went away again. Ben Tajah did not say anything to him about the letter. He wanted to drink the tea quietly and leave trouble until later.

When the muezzin called from the minaret of the Koutoubia, He of the Assembly thought of being in the Agdal. The great mountains were ahead of him and the olive trees stood in rows on each side of him. Then he heard the trickle of water and he remembered the *seguia* that is there in the Agdal, and he swiftly came back to the Café of the Two Bridges. Aïcha Qandicha can be only where there are trees

by running water. 'She comes only for single men by trees
and fresh moving water. Her arms are gold and she calls in
the voice of the most cherished one.' Ben Tajah gave him
the *sebsi*. He filled it and smoked it. 'When a man sees her
face he will never see another woman's face. He will make
love with her all the night, and every night, and in the sunlight by the walls, before the eyes of children. Soon he will
be an empty pod and he will leave this world for his home
in Jehennem.' The last carriage went by, taking the last
tourists down the road beside the ramparts to their rooms
in the Mamounia. He of the Assembly thought : 'The eye
wants to sleep. But this man is alone in the world. He wants
to talk all night. He wants to tell me about his wife and
how he beat her and how she broke everything. Why do I
want to know all those things? He is a good man but he has
no head.' Ben Tajah was sad. He said : 'What have I done?
Why does Satan choose me?' Then at last he told the boy
about the letter, about how he wondered if it had had his
name on the envelope and how he was not even sure there
had been a letter. When he finished he looked sadly at the
boy. 'And you didn't see me.' He of the Assembly shut his
eyes and kept them shut for a while. When he opened them
again he said : 'Are you alone in the world?' Ben Tajah
stared at him and did not speak. The boy laughed. 'I did
see you,' he said, 'but you had no letter. I saw you when
you were getting up and I thought you were old. Then I
saw you were not old. That's all I saw.' 'No, it isn't,' Ben
Tajah said. 'You saw I was alone.' He of the Assembly
shrugged. 'Who knows?' He filled the *sebsi* and handed it to
Ben Tajah. The kif was in Ben Tajah's head. His eyes were
small. He of the Assembly listened to the wind in the telephone wires, took back the *sebsi* and filled it again. Then
he said : 'You think Satan is coming to make trouble for

you because you're alone in the world. I see that. Get a
wife or somebody to be with you always, and you won't
think about it any more. That's true. Because Satan doesn't
come to men like you.' He of the Assembly did not believe
this himself. He knew that Father Satan can come for anyone in the world, but he hoped to live with Ben Tajah, so
he would not have to borrow money in the *souks* to buy
food. Ben Tajah drank some tea. He did not want the boy to
see that his face was happy. He felt that the boy was right,
and that there never had been a letter. 'Two days on a bus
is a long time. A man can get very tired,' he said. Then he
called the *qahouaji* and told him to bring two more glasses
of tea. He of the Assembly gave him the *sebsi*. He knew
that Ben Tajah wanted to stay as long as possible in the
Café of the Two Bridges. He put his finger into the *mottoui*.
The kif was almost gone. 'We can talk,' he said. 'Not much
kif is in the *mottoui*.' The *qahouaji* brought the tea. They
talked for an hour or more. The *qahouaji* slept and snored.
They talked about Satan and the bad thing it is to live
alone, to wake up in the dark and know that there is no one
else nearby. Many times He of the Assembly told Ben
Tajah that he must not worry. The kif was all gone. He
held his empty *mottoui* in his hand. He did not understand
how he had got back to the town without climbing up out
of the soup kettle. Once he said to Ben Tajah : 'I never
climbed back up.' Ben Tajah looked at him and said he did
not understand. He of the Assembly told him the story. Ben
Tajah laughed. He said : 'You smoke too much kif, brother.'
He of the Assembly put his *sebsi* into his pocket. 'And you
don't smoke and you're afraid of Satan,' he told Ben Tajah.
'No!' Ben Tajah shouted. 'By Allah ! No more! But one
thing is in my head, and I can't put it out. The sky trembles
and the earth is afraid, and the two eyes are not brothers.

Did you ever hear those words? Where did they come from?' Ben Tajah looked hard at the boy. He of the Assembly understood that these had been the words on the paper, and he felt cold in the middle of his back because he had never heard them before and they sounded evil. He knew, too, that he must not let Ben Tajah know this. He began to laugh. Ben Tajah took hold of his knee and shook it. His face was troubled. 'Did you ever hear them?' He of the Assembly went on laughing. Ben Tajah shook his leg so hard that he stopped and said : 'Yes!' When Ben Tajah waited and he said nothing more, he saw the man's face growing angry, and so he said : 'Yes, I've heard them. But will you tell me what happened to me and how I got out of the soup-kettle if I tell you about those words?' Ben Tajah understood that the kif was going away from the boy's head. But he saw that it had not all gone, or he would not have been asking that question. And he said : 'Wait a while for the answer to that question.' He of the Assembly woke the *qahouaji* and Ben Tajah paid him, and they went out of the café. They did not talk while they walked. When they got to the Mouassine mosque, Ben Tajah held out his hand to say goodnight, but He of the Assembly said : 'I'm looking in my head for the place I heard your words. I'll walk to your door with you. Maybe I'll remember.' Ben Tajah said : 'May Allah help you find it.' And he took his arm and they walked to Ben Tajah's door while He of the Assembly said nothing. They stood outside the door in the dark. 'Have you found it?' said Ben Tajah. 'Almost,' said He of the Assembly. Ben Tajah thought that perhaps when the kif had gone out of the boy's head he might be able to tell him about the words. He wanted to know how the boy's head was, and so he said : 'Do you still want to know how you got out of the soup-kettle?' He of the Assembly laughed.

'You said you would tell me later,' he told Ben Tajah. 'I will,' said Ben Tajah. 'Come upstairs. Since we have to wait, we can sit down.' Ben Tajah opened the door and they went upstairs. This time He of the Assembly sat down on Ben Tajah's bed. He yawned and stretched. It was a good bed. He was glad it was not the mat by the bamboo fence at the Café of the Two Bridges. 'And so, tell me how I got out of the soup-kettle,' he said laughing. Ben Tajah said : 'You're still asking me that? Have you thought of the words?' 'I know the words,' the boy said. 'The sky trembles. . . .' Ben Tajah did not want him to say them again. 'Where did you hear them? What are they? That's what I want to know.' The boy shook his head. Then he sat up very straight and looked beyond Ben Tajah, beyond the wall of the room, beyond the streets of the Medina, beyond the gardens, toward the mountains where the people speak Tachelhait. He remembered being a little boy. 'This night is a jewel in my crown,' he thought. 'It went this way.' And he began to sing, making up a melody for the words Ben Tajah had told him. When he had finished '. . . and the two eyes are not brothers,' he added a few more words of his own and stopped singing. 'That's all I remember of the song,' he said. Ben Tajah clapped his hands together hard. 'A song !' he cried. 'I must have heard it on the radio.' He of the Assembly shrugged. 'They play it sometimes,' he said. 'I've made him happy,' he thought. 'But I won't ever tell him another lie. That's the only one. What I'm going to do now is not the same as lying.' He got up off the bed and went to the window. The muezzins were calling the *fjer*. 'It's almost morning,' he said to Ben Tajah. 'I still have kif in my head.' 'Sit down,' said Ben Tajah. He was sure now there had been no letter. He of the Assembly took off his *djellaba* and got into bed. Ben Tajah looked at

him in surprise. Then he undressed and got into bed beside
him. He left the candle burning on the floor beside the bed.
He meant to stay awake, but he went to sleep because he
was not used to smoking kif and the kif was in his head.
He of the Assembly did not believe he was asleep. He lay
for a long time without moving. He listened to the voices
of the muezzins, and he thought that the man beside him
would speak or move. When he saw that Ben Tajah was
surely asleep, he was angry. 'This is how he treats a friend
who has made him happy. He forgets his trouble and his
friend too.' He thought about it more and he was angrier.
The muezzins were still calling the *fjer*. 'Before they stop,
or he will hear.' Very slowly he got out of the bed. He put
on his *djellaba* and opened the door. Then he went back
and took all the money out of Ben Tajah's pockets. In with
the banknotes was an envelope that was folded. It had Ben
Tajah's name written across it. He pulled out the piece of
paper inside and held it near the candle, and then he looked
at it as he would have looked at a snake. The words were
written there. Ben Tajah's face was turned toward the wall
and he was snoring. He of the Assembly held the paper
above the flame and burned it, and then he burned the
envelope. He blew the black paper-ashes across the floor.
Without making any noise he ran downstairs and let himself out into the street. He shut the door. The money was in
his pocket and he walked fast to his aunt's house. His aunt
awoke and was angry for a while. Finally he said : 'It was
raining. How could I come home? Let me sleep.' He had
a little kif hidden under his pillow. He smoked a pipe. Then
he looked across his sleep to the morning and thought : 'A
pipe of kif before breakfast gives a man the strength of a
hundred camels in the courtyard.'

The Garden

A man who lived in a distant town of the southern country was working in his garden. Because he was poor his land was at the edge of the oasis. All the afternoon he dug channels, and when the day was finished he went to the upper end of the garden and opened the gate that held back the water. And now the water ran in the channels to the beds of barley and the young pomegranate trees. The sky was red, and when the man saw the floor of his garden shining like jewels, he sat down on a stone to look at it. As he watched, it grew brighter, and he thought: 'There is no finer garden in the oasis.'

A great happiness filled him, and he sat there a long time, and did not get home until very late. When he went into the house, his wife looked at him and saw the joy still in his eyes.

'He has found a treasure,' she thought; but she said nothing. When they sat face to face at the evening meal, the man was still remembering his garden, and it seemed to him that now that he had known this happiness, never again would he be without it. He was silent as he ate.

His wife too was silent. 'He is thinking of the treasure,' she said to herself. And she was angry, believing that he did not want to share his secret with her. The next morning she went to the house of an old woman and bought many herbs and powders from her. She took them home and passed several days mixing and cooking them, until she had made the medicine she wanted. Then at each meal she began to put a little of the *tsoukel* into her husband's food.

It was not long before the man fell ill. For a time he went each day to his garden to work, but often when he got there he was so weak that he could merely sit leaning against a palm tree. He had a sharp sound in his ears, and he could not follow his thoughts as they came to him. In spite of this, each day when the sun went down and he saw his garden shining red in its light, he was happy. And when he got home at night his wife could see that there was joy in his eyes.

'He has been counting the treasure,' she thought, and she began to go secretly to the garden to watch him from behind the trees. When she saw that he merely sat looking at the ground, she went back to the old woman and told her about it.

'You must hurry and make him talk, before he forgets where he has hidden the treasure,' said the old woman.

That night the wife put a great amount of *tsoukel* into his food, and when they were drinking tea afterward she began to say many sweet words to him. The man only smiled. She tried for a long time to make him speak, but he merely shrugged his shoulders and made motions with his hands.

The next morning while he was still asleep, she went back to the old woman and told her that the man could no longer speak.

'You have given him too much,' the old woman said. 'He will never tell you his secret now. The only thing for you to do is go away quickly, before he dies.'

The woman ran home. Her husband lay on the mat with

his mouth open. She packed her clothing and left the town that morning.

For three days the man lay in a deep sleep. The fourth day when he awoke, it was as if he had made a voyage to the other side of the world. He was very hungry, but all he could find in the house was a piece of dry bread. When he had eaten that, he walked to his garden at the edge of the oasis and picked many figs. Then he sat down and ate them. In his mind there was no thought of his wife, because he had forgotten her. When a neighbor came by and called to him, he answered politely, as if speaking to a stranger, and the neighbor went away perplexed.

Little by little the man grew healthy once more. He worked each day in the garden. When dusk came, after watching the sunset and the red water, he would go home and cook his dinner and sleep. He had no friends, because although men spoke to him, he did not know who they were, and he only smiled and nodded to them. Then the people in the town began to notice that he no longer went to the mosque to pray. They spoke about this among themselves, and one evening the imam went to the man's house to talk with him.

As they sat there, the imam listened for sounds of the man's wife in the house. Out of courtesy he could not mention her, but he was thinking about her and asking himself where she might be. He went away from the house full of doubts.

The man went on living his life. But the people of the town now talked of little else. They whispered that he had killed his wife, and many of them wanted to go together and search the house for her remains. The imam spoke against this idea, saying that he would go and talk again with the man. And this time he went all the way to the garden at

the edge of the oasis, and found him there working happily
with the plants and the trees. He watched him for a while,
and then he walked closer and spoke a few words with him.

It was late in the afternoon. The sun was sinking in the
west, and the water on the ground began to be red. Presently
the man said to the imam : 'The garden is beautiful.'

'Beautiful or not beautiful,' said the imam, 'you should
be giving thanks to Allah for allowing you to have it.'

'Allah?' said the man. 'Who is that? I never heard of
him. I made this garden myself. I dug every channel and
planted every tree, and no one helped me. I have no debts
to anyone.'

The imam had turned pale. He flung out his arm and
struck the man very hard in the face. Then he went quickly
out of the garden.

The man stood with his hand to his cheek. 'He has gone
mad,' he thought, as the imam walked away.

That night the people spoke together in the mosque. They
decided that the man could no longer live in their town.
Early the next morning a great crowd of men, with the
imam going at the head of it, went out into the oasis, on its
way to the man's garden.

The small boys ran ahead of the men, and got there long
before them. They hid in the bushes, and as the man worked
they began to throw stones and shout insults at him. He
paid no attention to them. Then a stone hit the back of his
head. He jumped up quickly. As they ran away, one of
them fell, and the man caught him. He tried to hold him
still so he could ask him : 'Why were you throwing stones
at me?' But the boy only screamed and struggled.

And the townspeople, who were on their way, heard the
screaming, and they came running to the garden. They
pulled the boy away from him and began to strike at the

man with hoes and sickles. When they had destroyed him, they left him there with his head lying in one of the channels, and went back to the town, giving thanks to Allah that the boy was safe.

Little by little the sand covered everything. The trees died, and very soon the garden was gone. Only the desert was there.

The Story of Lahcen and Idir

Two friends, Lahcen and Idir, were walking on the beach at Merkala. By the rocks stood a girl, and her *djellaba* blew in the wind. Lahcen and Idir stopped walking when they saw her. They stood still, looking at her. Lahcen said : 'Do you know that one?' 'No. I never saw her.' 'Let's go over,' said Lahcen. They looked up and down the beach for a man who might be with the girl, but there was no one. 'A whore,' said Lahcen. When they got closer to the girl, they saw that she was very young. Lahcen laughed. 'This is easy.' 'How much have you got?' Idir asked him. 'You think I'm going to pay her?' cried Lahcen.

Idir understood that Lahcen meant to beat her. ('If you don't pay a whore you have to beat her.') And he did not like the idea, because they had done it before together, and it nearly always meant trouble later. Her sister or someone in her family went to the police and complained, and in the end everybody was in jail. Being shut into prison made Idir nervous. He tried to keep out of it, and he was usually able to. The difference between Lahcen and Idir was that Lahcen liked to drink and Idir smoked kif. Kif smokers want to stay quiet in their heads, and drinkers are not like that. They want to break things.

Lahcen rubbed his groin and spat onto the sand. Idir knew he was going over the moves in the game he was going to play with the girl, planning when and where he would

knock her down. He was worried. The girl looked the other
way. She held down the skirt of her *djellaba* so the wind
would not blow it. Lahcen said : 'Wait here.' He went on
to her and Idir saw her lips moving as she spoke to him, for
she wore no veil. All her teeth were gold. Idir hated women
with gold teeth because at fourteen he had been in love with
a gold-toothed whore named Zohra, who never had paid
him any attention. He said to himself : 'He can have her.'
Besides, he did not want to be with them when the trouble
began. He stood still until Lahcen whistled to him. Then
he went over to where they stood. 'Ready?' Lahcen asked.
He took the girl's arm and started to walk along beside the
rocks. 'It's late. I've got to go,' Idir told him. Lahcen looked
surprised, but he said nothing. 'Some other day,' Idir told
Lahcen, looking at him and trying to warn him. The girl
laughed spitefully, as if she thought that might shame him
into coming along.

He was glad he had decided to go home. When he went
by the Mendoub's fig orchard a dog barked at him. He
threw a rock at it and hit it.

The next morning Lahcen came to Idir's room. His eyes
were red from the wine he had been drinking. He sat down
on the floor and pulled out a handkerchief that had a knot
tied in one corner. He untied the knot and let a gold ring
fall out into his lap. Picking up the ring, he handed it to
Idir. 'For you. I got it cheap.' Idir saw that Lahcen wanted
him to take the ring, and he put it on his finger, saying :
'May Allah give you health.' Lahcen rubbed his hand across
his chin and yawned. Then he said : 'I saw you look at me,
and afterward when we got to the quarry I thought that
would be the best place. And then I remembered the night the
police took us at Bou Khach Khach, and I remembered you
looking at me. I turned around left her there. Garbage !'

'So you're not in jail and you're drunk,' said Idir, and he laughed.

'That's true,' said Lahcen. 'And that's why I give you the ring.'

Idir knew the ring was worth at least fifty dirhams, and he could sell it if he needed money badly. That would end his friendship with Lahcen, but there would be no help for it.

Sometimes Lahcen came by in the evening with a bottle of wine. He would drink the whole bottle while Idir smoked his kif pipe, and they would listen to the radio until the end of the program at twelve o'clock. Afterward, very late, they would walk through the streets of Dradeb to a garage where a friend of Lahcen's was night watchman. When the moon was full, it was brighter than the street lights. With no moon, there was nobody in the streets, and in the few late cafés the men told one another about what thieves had done, and how there were more of them than ever before. This was because there was almost no work to be had anywhere, and the country people were selling their cows and sheep to be able to pay their taxes, and then coming to the city. Lahcen and Idir worked now and then, whenever they found something to do. They had a little money, they always ate, and Lahcen sometimes was able to afford his bottle of Spanish wine. Idir's kif was more of a problem, because each time the police decided to enforce the law they had made against it, it grew very scarce and the price went up. Then when there was plenty to be had, because the police were busy looking for guns and rebels instead, the price stayed high. He did not smoke any less, but he smoked by himself in his room. If you smoke in a café, there is always someone who has left his kif at home and wants to use yours. He told his friends at the Café Nadjah that he had given up kif, and he never accepted a pipe when it was offered to him.

Back in his room in the early evening, with the window open and the sleepy sounds of the town coming up, for it was summer and the voices of people filled the streets, Idir sat in the chair he had bought and put his feet on the windowsill. That way he could see the sky as he smoked. Lahcen would come in and talk. Now and then they went together to Emsallah to a *barraca* there near the slaughter house where two sisters lived with their feeble-minded mother. They would get the mother drunk and put her to bed in the inner room. Then they would get the girls drunk and spend the night with them, without paying. The cognac was expensive, but it did not cost as much as whores would have.

In midsummer, at the time of Sidi Kacem, it suddenly grew very hot. People set up tents made of sheets on the roofs of their houses and cooked and slept there. At night in the moonlight Idir could see all the roofs, each one with its box of sheets flapping in the wind, and inside the sheets the red light made by the fire in the pot. Daytimes, the sun shining on the sea of white sheets hurt his eyes, and he remembered not to look out when he passed the window as he moved about his room. He would have liked to live in a more expensive room, one with a blind to keep out the light. There was no way of being protected from the bright summer day that filled the sky outside, and he waited with longing for dusk. His custom was not to smoke kif before the sun went down. He did not like it in the daytime, above all in summer when the air is hot and the light is powerful. When each day came up hotter than the one before it, he decided to buy enough food and kif to last several days, and to shut himself into his room until it got cooler. He had

worked two days at the port that week and had some
money. He put the food on the table and locked the door.
Then he took the key out of the lock and threw it into the
drawer of the table. Lying with the packages and cans in
his market basket was a large bundle of kif wrapped in a
newspaper. He unfolded it, took out a sheaf and sniffed
at it. For the next two hours he sat on the floor picking off
the leaves and cutting them on a breadboard, sifting, and
cutting, again and again. Once, as the sun reached him, he
had to move to get out of its heat. By the time the sun
went down he had enough ready for three or four days. He
got up off the floor and sat in his chair with his pouch and
his pipe in his lap, and smoked, while the radio played the
Chleuh music that was always broadcast at this hour for
the Soussi shopkeepers. In cafés men often got up and
turned it off. Idir enjoyed it. Kif smokers usually like it,
because of the *naqous* that always pounds the same design.

The music played a long time, and Idir thought of the
market at Tiznit and the mosque with the tree trunks stick-
ing out of its mud walls. He looked down the floor. The
room still had daylight in it. He opened his eyes wide. A
small bird was walking slowly along the floor. He jumped
up. The kif pipe fell, but its bowl did not break. Before the
bird had time to move, he had put his hand over it. Even
when he held it between his two hands it did not struggle.
He looked at it, and thought it was the smallest bird he
had ever seen. Its head was gray, and its wings were black
and white. It looked at him, and it did not seem afraid. He
sat down in the chair with the bird in his lap. When he lifted
his hand it stayed still. 'It's a young bird and can't fly,' he
thought. He smoked several pipes of kif. The bird did not
move. The sun had gone down and the houses were growing
blue in the evening light. He stroked the bird's head with

his thumb. Then he took the ring from his little finger and slipped it over the smooth feathers of its head. The bird paid no attention. 'A gold collar for the sultan of birds,' he said. He smoked some more kif and looked at the sky. Then he began to be hungry, and he thought the bird might like some breadcrumbs. He put his pipe down on the table and tried to take the ring from the bird's head. It would not come off over the feathers. He pulled at it, and the bird fluttered its wings and struggled. For a second he let go of it, and in that instant it flew straight from his lap into the sky. Idir jumped up and stood watching it. When it was gone, he began to smile. 'The son of a whore!' he whispered.

He prepared his food and ate it. After that he sat in the chair smoking and thinking about the bird. When Lahcen came he told him the story. 'He was waiting all the time for a chance to steal something,' he said. Lahcen was a little drunk, and he was angry. 'So he stole my ring!' he cried. 'Ah,' said Idir. 'Yours? I thought you gave it to me.'

'I'm not crazy yet,' Lahcen told him. He went away still angry, and did not return for more than a week. The morning he came into the room Idir was certain that he was going to begin to talk again about the ring, and he quickly handed him a pair of shoes he had bought from a friend the day before. 'Do these fit you?' he asked him. Lahcen sat down in the chair, put them on, and found they did fit. 'They need new bottoms, but the tops are like new,' Idir told him. 'The tops are good,' said Lahcen. He felt of the leather and squeezed it between his thumb and fingers. 'Take them,' said Idir. Lahcen was pleased, and he said nothing about the ring that day. When he got the shoes to his room he looked carefully at them and decided to spend the money that it would cost to have new soles made.

The next day he went to a Spanish cobbler, who agreed

to repair the shoes for fifteen dirhams. 'Ten,' said Lahcen.
After a long discussion the cobbler lowered his price to
thirteen, and he left the shoes there, saying that he would
call for them in a week. The same afternoon he was walking through Sidi Bouknadel, and he saw a girl. They talked
together for two hours or more, standing not very near to
each other beside the wall, and looking down at the ground
so that no one could see they were talking. The girl was
from Meknes, and that was why he had never seen her
before. She was visiting her aunt, who lived there in the
quarter, and soon her sister was coming from Meknes. She
looked to him the best thing he had seen that year, but of
course he could not be sure of her nose and mouth because
her veil hid them. He got her to agree to meet him at the
same place the next day. This time they took a walk along
the Hafa, and he could see that she would be willing. But
she would not tell him where her aunt's house was.

Only two days later he got her to his room. As he had
expected, she was beautiful. That night he was very happy.
but in the morning when she had gone, he understood that
he wanted to be with her all the time. He wanted to know
what her aunt's house was like and how she was going to
pass her day. In this way a bad time began for Lahcen. He
was happy only when she was with him and he could get
into bed and see her lying on one side of him and a bottle
of cognac on the other, upright on the floor beside his pillow, where he could reach it easily. Each day when she had
gone he lay thinking about all the men she might be going
to see before she came back to him. When he talked about
it to her she laughed and said she spent all her time with
her aunt and sister, who now had arrived from Meknes. But
he could not stop worrying about it.

Two weeks went by before he remembered to go and get

his shoes. On his way to the cobbler's he thought about how he would solve his problem. He had an idea that Idir could help him. If he brought Idir and the girl together and left them alone, Idir would tell him afterward everything that had happened. If she let Idir take her to bed, then she was a whore and could be treated like a whore. He would give her a good beating and then make it up with her, because she was too good to throw away. But he had to know whether she was really his, or whether she would go with others.

When the cobbler handed him his shoes, he saw that they looked almost like new, and he was pleased. He paid the thirteen dirhams and took the shoes home. That night when he was going to put them on to wear to the café, he found that his feet would not go into them. They were much too small. The cobbler had cut down the last in order to stitch on the new soles. He put his old shoes back on, went out, and slammed the door. That night he had a quarrel with the girl. It took him until almost dawn to stop her crying. When the sun came up and she was asleep, he lay with his arms folded behind his head looking at the ceiling, thinking that the shoes had cost him thirteen dirhams and now he was going to have to spend the day trying to sell them. He got rid of the girl early and went in to Bou Araqia with the shoes. No one would give him more than eight dirhams for them. In the afternoon he went to the Joteya and sat in the shade of a grapevine, waiting for the buyers and sellers to arrive. A man from the mountains finally offered him ten dirhams, and he sold the shoes. 'Three dirhams gone for nothing,' he thought when he put the money into his pocket. He was angry, but instead of blaming the cobbler, he felt that the fault was Idir's.

That afternoon he saw Idir, and he told him he would

bring a friend with him to Idir's room after the evening meal. Then he went home and drank cognac. When the girl arrived he had finished the bottle, and he was drunk and more unhappy than ever. 'Don't take it off,' he told her when she began to unfasten her veil. 'We're going out.' She said nothing. They took the back streets to Idir's room.

Idir sat in his chair listening to the radio. He had not expected a girl, and when he saw her take off her veil the beating of his heart made his head ache. He told her to sit in the chair, and then he paid no more attention to her and sat on the bed talking only with Lahcen, who did not look at her either. Soon Lahcen got up. 'I'm going out to get some cigarettes,' he said. 'I'll be right back.' He shut the door after him, and Idir quickly went and locked it. He smiled at the girl and sat on the table beside her, looking down at her. Now and then he smoked a pipe of kif. He wondered why Lahcen was taking so long. Finally he said : 'He's not coming back, you know.' The girl laughed and shrugged. He jumped up, took her hand, and led her to the bed.

In the morning when they were getting dressed, she told him she lived at the Hotel Sevilla. It was a small Moslem hotel in the center of the Medina. He took her there and left her. 'Will you come tonight?' she asked him. Idir frowned. He was thinking of Lahcen. 'Don't wait for me after midnight,' he said. On his way home he stopped at the Café Nadjah. Lahcen was there. His eyes were red and he looked as though he had not slept at all. Idir had the feeling that he had been waiting for him to appear, for when he came into the café Lahcen quickly got up and paid the *qahouaji*. They walked down the main street of Dradeb without saying anything, and when they got to the road that leads to the Merkala beach, they turned down it, still without speaking.

It was low tide. They walked on the wet sand while the small waves broke at their feet. Lahcen smoked a cigarette and threw stones into the water. Finally he spoke. 'How was it?'

Idir shrugged, tried to keep his voice flat. 'All right for one night,' he said. Lahcen was ready to say carelessly: 'Or even two.' But then he realized that Idir did not want to talk about the night, which meant that it had been a great event for him. And when he looked at his face he was certain that Idir wanted the girl for himself. He was sure he had already lost her to him, but he did not know why he had not thought of that in the beginning. Now he forgot the true reason why he had wanted to take her to Idir.

'You thought I brought her just to be good to you!' he cried. 'No, sidi! I left her there to see if you were a friend. And I see what kind of friend you are! A scorpion!' He seized the front of Idir's garments and struck him in the face. Idir moved backward a few steps, and got ready to fight. He understood that Lahcen had seen the truth, and that now there was nothing at all to say, and nothing to do but fight. When they were both bloody and panting, he looked for a flash at Lahcen's face, and saw that he was dizzy and could not see very well. He drew back, put his head down, and with all his force ran into Lahcen, who lost his balance and fell onto the sand. Then quickly he kicked him in the head with the heel of his shoe. He left him lying there and went home.

In a little while Lahcen began to hear the waves breaking on the sand near him. 'I must kill him,' he thought. 'He sold my ring. Now I must go and kill him.' Instead, he took

off his clothes and bathed in the sea, and when he had
finished, he lay in the sun on the sand all day and slept. In
the evening he went and got very drunk.

At eleven o'clock Idir went to the Hotel Sevilla. The girl
was sitting in a wicker chair by the front door, waiting for
him. She looked carefully at the cuts on his face. Under her
veil he saw her smile.

'You fought?' Idir nodded his head. 'How is he?' He
shrugged. This made her laugh. 'He was always drunk, anyway,' she said. Idir took her arm, and they went out into
the street.

The Delicate Prey

There were three Filala who sold leather in Tabelbala—
two brothers and the young son of their sister. The two
older merchants were serious, bearded men who liked to
engage in complicated theological discussions during the
slow passage of the hot hours in their *hanoute* near the
market-place; the youth naturally occupied himself almost
exclusively with the black-skinned girls in the small *quartier
réservé*. There was one who seemed more desirable than
the others, so that he was a little sorry when the older men
announced that soon they would all leave for Tessalit. But
nearly every town has its *quartier*, and Driss was reason-
ably certain of being able to have any lovely resident of
any *quartier*, whatever her present emotional entanglements;
thus his chagrin at hearing of the projected departure was
short-lived.

The three Filala waited for the cold weather before starting out for Tessalit. Because they wanted to get there quickly
they chose the westernmost trail, which is also the one
leading through the most remote regions, contiguous to the
lands of the plundering Reguibat tribes. It had been a long
time since the uncouth men from the uplands had swept
down from the *hammada* upon a caravan; most people were
of the opinion that since the war of the Sarrho they had lost
the greater part of their arms and ammunition, and, more
important still, their spirit. And a tiny group of three men

117

and their camels could scarcely awaken the envy of the Reguibat, traditionally rich with loot from all Rio de Oro and Mauretania.

Their friends in Tabelbala, most of them other Filali leather merchants, walked beside them sadly as far as the edge of the town; then they bade them farewell, and watched them mount their camels to ride off slowly toward the bright horizon.

'If you meet any Reguibat, keep them ahead of you!' they called.

The danger lay principally in the territory they would reach only three or four days' journey from Tabelbala; after a week the edge of the land haunted by the Reguibat would be left entirely behind. The weather was cool save at midday. They took turns sitting guard at night; when Driss stayed awake he brought out a small flute whose piercing notes made the older uncle frown with annoyance, so that he asked him to go and sit at some distance from the sleeping-blankets. All night he sat playing whatever sad songs he could call to mind; the bright ones in his opinion belonged to the *quartier*, where one was never alone.

When the uncles kept watch, they sat quietly, staring ahead of them into the night. There were just the three of them.

And then one day a solitary figure appeared, moving toward them across the lifeless plains from the west. One man on a camel; there was no sign of any others, although they scanned the wasteland in every direction. They stopped for a while; he altered his course slightly. They went ahead; he changed it again. There was no doubt that he wanted to speak with them.

'Let him come,' grumbled the older uncle, glaring about the empty horizon once more. 'We each have a gun.'

Driss laughed. To him it seemed absurd even to admit the possibility of trouble from one lone man.

When finally the figure arrived within calling distance, it hailed them in a voice like a muezzin's : *'S'l'm aleikoum!'* They halted, but did not dismount, and waited for the man to draw nearer. Soon he called again. This time the uncle replied, but the distance was still too great for his voice to carry, and the man did not hear his greeting. Presently he was close enough for them to see that he did not wear Reguiba attire. They muttered to one another : 'He comes from the north, not the west.' And they all felt glad. However, even when he came up beside them they remained on the camels, bowing solemnly from where they sat and always searching in the new face, and in the garments below it, for some false note which might reveal the possible truth—that the man was a scout for the Reguibat, who would be waiting up on the *hammada* only a few hours distant, or were even now moving parallel to the trail, closing in upon them in such a manner that they would not arrive at a point within visibility until after dusk.

Certainly the stranger himself was no Reguiba. He was quick and jolly, with light skin and very little beard. It occurred to Driss that he did not like his small, active eyes which seemed to take in everything and give out nothing, but this passing reaction became only a part of the general initial distrust, all of which was dissipated when they learned that the man was a Moungari. Moungar is a holy place in that part of the world, and its few residents are treated with respect by the pilgrims who go to visit the ruined shrine nearby.

The newcomer took no pains to hide the fear he had felt at being alone in the region, or the pleasure it gave him to be now with three other men. They all dismounted and made tea to seal their friendship, the Moungari furnishing the charcoal.

During the third round of glasses he made the suggestion that, since he was going more or less in their direction, he accompany them as far as Taoudeni. His bright black eyes darting from one Filali to the other, he explained that he was an excellent shot; he was certain he could supply them all with some good gazelle meat en route, or at least an *aoudad*. The Filala considered; the oldest finally said. 'Agreed.' Even if the Moungari turned out to have not quite the hunting prowess he claimed for himself, there would be four of them on the voyage instead of three.

Two mornings later, in the mighty silence of the rising sun, the Moungari pointed at the low hills that lay beside them to the east. '*Timma*. I know this land. Wait here. If you hear me shoot, then come, because that will mean there are gazelles.'

The Moungari went off on foot, climbing up between the boulders and disappearing behind the nearest crest. 'He trusts us,' thought the Filala. 'He has left his *mehari*, his blankets, his packs.' They said nothing, but each knew that the others were thinking the same as he, and they all felt warmly toward this stranger. They sat waiting in the early morning chill while the camels grumbled.

It seemed unlikely that there would prove to be any gazelles in the region, but if there should be any, and the Moungari were as good a hunter as he claimed to be, then there was a chance they would have a *mechoui* of gazelle that evening, and that would be very fine.

Slowly the sun mounted in the hard blue sky. One camel lumbered up and went off, hoping to find a dead thistle or a bush between the rocks, something left over from a year when rain may have fallen. When it had disappeared, Driss

went in search of it and drove it back to the others, shouting *'Hut!'*

He sat down. Suddenly there came a shot, a long empty
interval, and then another shot. The sounds were fairly
distant, but perfectly clear in the absolute silence. The older
brother said : 'I shall go. Who knows? There may be many
gazelles.' He clambered up the rocks, the gun in his hand,
and was gone.

Again they waited. When the shots sounded this time,
they came from two guns.

'Perhaps they have killed one!' Driss cried.

'Yemkin. With Allah's aid,' replied his uncle, rising and
taking up his gun. 'I want to try my hand at this.'

Driss was disappointed : he had hoped to go himself. If
only he had got up a moment ago it might have been possible, but even so it was likely that he would have been
left behind to watch the *mehara.* In any case, now it was
too late; his uncle had spoken.

'Good.'

His uncle went off singing a song from Tafilalet, about
date-palms and hidden smiles. For several minutes Driss
heard snatches of the song as the melody reached the high
notes. Then the sound was lost in the enveloping silence.

He waited. The sun was becoming very hot. He covered
his head with his burnoose. The camels looked at each other
stupidly, craning their necks, baring their brown and yellow
teeth. He thought of playing his flute, but it did not seem
the right moment : he was too restless, too eager to be up
there with his gun, crouching behind the rocks, stalking the
delicate prey. He thought of Tessalit and wondered what it
would be like. Full of Blacks and Touareg, certainly more
lively than Tabelbala because of the road that passed
through it. There was a shot. He waited for others, but no

more came this time. Again he imagined himself there
among the boulders, taking aim at a fleeing beast. He pulled
the trigger, the animal fell. Others appeared, and he got
them all. In the dark the travelers sat around the fire gorg-
ing themselves with the rich roasted flesh, their faces gleam-
ing with grease. Everyone was happy, and even the Mou-
gari admitted that the young Filali was the best hunter of
them all.

In the advancing heat he dozed, his mind playing over a
landscape made of soft thighs and small hard breasts rising
like sand dunes; wisps of song floated like clouds in the sky,
and the air was thick with the taste of fat gazelle meat.

He sat up and looked around quickly. The camels lay
with their necks stretched along the ground in front of
them. Nothing had changed. He stood up, uneasily scanning
the stony landscape. While he had slept, a hostile presence
had entered into his consciousness. Translating into thought
what he already sensed, he cried out. Since first he had seen
those small, active eyes he had felt mistrustful of their
owner, but the fact that his uncles had accepted him had
pushed suspicion away into the dark of his mind. Now, un-
leashed in slumber, it had bounded back. He turned toward
the hot hillside and looked intently between the boulders
into the black shadows. In memory he heard again the shots
up among the rocks, and he knew what they had meant.
Catching his breath in a sob, he ran to mount his *mehari*,
forced it up, and already had gone several hundred paces
before he was aware of what he was doing. He stopped the
animal and sat quietly a moment, glacing back at the camp-
site with fear and indecision. If his uncles were dead, then
there was nothing to do but get out into the open desert as
quickly as possible, away from the rocks that could hide the
Moungari while he took aim.

And so, not knowing the way to Tessalit, and without sufficient food or water, he started ahead, lifting one hand from time to time to wipe away the tears.

For two or three hours he continued that way, scarcely noticing where the *mehari* walked. All at once he sat erect, uttered an oath against himself, and in a fury turned the beast around. At that very moment his uncles might be seated in the camp with the Moungari, preparing a *mechoui* and a fire, sadly asking themselves why their nephew had deserted them. Or perhaps one would already have set out in search of him. There would be no possible excuse for his conduct, which had been the result of an absurd terror. As he thought about it, his anger against himself mounted : he had behaved in an unforgivable manner. Noon had passed; the sun was in the west. It would be late when he got back. At the prospect of the inevitable reproaches and the mocking laughter that would greet him, he felt his face grow hot with shame, and he kicked the *mehari's* flanks viciously.

A good while before he arrived at the camp he heard singing. This surprised him. He halted and listened : the voice was too far away to be identified, but Driss felt certain it was the Moungari's. He continued around the side of the hill to a spot in full view of the camels. The singing stopped, leaving silence. Some of the packs had been loaded back on to the beasts, preparatory to setting out. The sun had sunk low, and the shadows of the rocks were stretched out along the earth. There was no sign that they had caught any game. He called out, ready to dismount. Almost at the same instant there was a shot from very nearby, and he heard the small rushing sound of a bullet go past his head. He seized his gun. There was another shot, a sharp pain in his arm, and his gun slipped to the ground.

For a moment he sat there holding his arm, dazed. Then
swiftly he leapt down and remained crouching among the
stones, reaching out with his good arm for the gun. As he
touched it, there was a third shot, and the rifle moved along
the ground a few inches toward him in a small cloud of dust.
He drew back his hand and looked at it : it was dark and
blood dripped from it. At that moment the Moungari
bounded across the open space between them. Before Driss
could rise the man was upon him, had pushed him back
down to the ground with the barrel of his rifle. The un-
troubled sky lay above; the Moungari glanced up at it
defiantly. He straddled the supine youth, thrusting the gun
into his neck just below the chin, and under his breath he
said : 'Filali dog !'

Driss stared up at him with a certain curiosity. The
Moungari had the upper hand; Driss could only wait. He
looked at the face in the sun's light, and discovered a
peculiar intensity there. He knew the expression : it comes
from hashish. Carried along on its hot fumes, a man can
escape very far from the world of meaning. To avoid the
malevolent face he rolled his eyes from side to side. There
was only the fading sky. The gun was choking him a little.
He whispered : 'Where are my uncles ?'

The Moungari pushed harder against his throat with
the gun, leaned partially over and with one hand ripped
away his *serouelle*, so that he lay naked from the waist
down, squirming a little as he felt the cold stones beneath
him.

Then the Moungari drew forth rope and bound his feet.
Taking two steps to his head, he abruptly faced in the other
direction, and thrust the gun into his navel. Still with one
hand, he slipped the remaining garments off over the youth's
head and lashed his wrists together. With an old barber's

razor he cut off the superfluous rope. During this time Driss called his uncles by name, loudly, first one and then the other.

The man moved and surveyed the young body lying on the stones. He ran his finger along the razor's blade; a pleasant excitement took possession of him. He stepped over, looked down, and saw the sex that sprouted from the base of the belly. Not entirely conscious of what he was doing, he took it in one hand and brought his other arm down with the motion of a reaper wielding a sickle. It was swiftly severed. A round, dark hole was left, flush with the skin; he stared a moment, blankly. Driss was screaming. The muscles all over his body stood out, moved.

Slowly the Moungari smiled, showing his teeth. He put his hand on the hard belly and smoothed the skin. Then he made a small vertical incision there, and using both hands, studiously stuffed the loose organ in until it disappeared.

As he was cleaning his hands in the sand, one of the camels uttered a sudden growling gurgle. The Moungari leapt up and wheeled about savagely, holding his razor high in the air. Then, ashamed of his nervousness, feeling that Driss was watching and mocking him (although the youth's eyes were unseeing with pain), he kicked him over onto his stomach where he lay making small spasmodic movements. And as the Moungari followed these with his eyes, a new idea came to him. It would be pleasant to inflict an ultimate indignity upon the young Filali. He threw himself down; this time he was vociferous and leisurely in his enjoyment. Eventually he slept.

At dawn he awoke and reached for his razor, lying on the ground nearby. Driss moaned faintly. The Moungari turned him over and pushed the blade back and forth with a sawing motion into his neck, until he was certain he had severed the windpipe. Then he rose, walked away, and finished the loading of the camels he had started the day before. When this was done he spent a good while dragging the body over to the base of the hill and concealing it there among the rocks.

In order to transport the Filala's merchandise to Tessalit (for in Taoudeni there would be no buyers), it was necessary to take their *mehara* with him. It was nearly fifty days later when he arrived. Tessalit is a small town. When the Moungari began to show the leather around, an old Filali living there, whom the people called Ech Chibani, got wind of his presence. As a prospective buyer he came to examine the hides, and the Moungari was unwise enough to let him see them. Filali leather is unmistakable, and only the Filala buy and sell it in quantity. Ech Chibani knew the Moungari had come by it illicitly, but he said nothing. When a few days later another caravan arrived from Tabelbala with friends of the three Filala who asked after them, and showed great distress on hearing that they never had arrived, the old man went to the Tribunal. After some difficulty, he found a Frenchman who was willing to listen to him. The next day the Commandant and two subordinates paid the Moungari a visit. They asked him how he happened to have the three extra *mehara*, which still carried some of their Filali trappings; his replies took a devious turn. The Frenchmen listened seriously, thanked him, and left. He did not see the Commandant wink at the others as they went out into the street. And so he remained sitting in his courtyard, not knowing that he had been judged and found guilty.

The three Frenchmen went back to the Tribunal where the newly arrived Filali merchants were sitting with Ech Chibani. The story had an old pattern; there was no doubt

at all about the Moungari's guilt. 'He is yours,' said the
Commandant. 'Do what you like with him.'

The Filala thanked him profusely, held a short conference
with the aged Chibani, and strode out in a group. When
they arrived at the Moungari's dwelling he was making tea.
He looked up, and a chill moved along his spine. He began
to scream his innocence at them; they said nothing, but at
the point of a rifle bound him and tossed him into a corner,
where he continued to babble and sob. Quietly, they drank
the tea he had been brewing, made some more, and went
out at twilight. They tied him to one of the *mehara*, and
mounting their own, moved in a silent procession (silent save
for the Moungari) out through the town gate into the in-
finite wasteland beyond.

Half the night they continued, until they were in a completely unfrequented region of the desert. While he lay
raving, bound to the camel, they dug a well-like pit, and
when they had finished they lifted him off, still trussed
tightly, and stood him in it. Then they filled all the space
around his body with sand and stones, until only his head
remained above the earth's surface. In the faint light of the
new moon his shaved pate without its turban looked rather
like a rock. And still he pleaded with them, calling upon
Allah and Sidi Ahmed ben Moussa to witness his innocence.
But he might have been singing a song for all the attention
they paid to his words. Presently they set off for Tessalit; in
no time they were out of hearing.

When they had gone the Moungari fell silent, to wait
through the cold hours for the sun that would bring first
warmth, then heat, thirst, fire, visions. The next night he
did not know where he was, did not feel the cold. The wind
blew dust along the ground into his mouth as he sang.

A Friend of the World

Salam rented two rooms and a kitchen on the second floor of a Jewish house at the edge of the town. He had decided to live with the Jews because he had already lived with Christians and found them all right. He trusted them a little more than he did other Moslems, who were like him and said : 'No Moslem can be trusted.' Moslems are the only true people, the only people you can understand. But because you do understand them, you do not trust them. Salam did not trust the Jews completely, either, but he liked living with them because they paid no attention to him. It had no importance if they talked about him among themselves, and they never would talk about him to Moslems. If he had a sister who lived here and there, getting what money she could from whatever man she found, because she had to eat, that was all right, and the Jews did not point at her when she came to visit him. If he did not get married, but lived instead with his brother and spent his time smoking kif and laughing, if he got his money by going to Tangier once a month and sleeping for a week with old English and American ladies who drank too much whisky, they did not care. He was a Moslem. Had he been rich he would have lived in the Spanish end of the town in a villa with concrete benches in the garden and a big round light in the ceiling of the *sala*, with many pieces of glass hanging down from it. He was poor and he lived with the Jews. To get to his house he had to go to the end of the Medina, cross an open space where the trees had all been cut down, go along the street where the warehouses had been abandoned by the Spanish when they left, and into a newer, dirtier street that led to the main highway. Halfway down was the entrance to the alley where he and his brother and fourteen Jewish families lived. There were the remains of narrow sidewalks along the edges of the wide gutter, full of mounds of rotten watermelon-rind and piles of broken bricks. The small children played here all day. When he was in a hurry he had to be careful not to step on them as they waded in the little puddles of dishwater and urine that were in front of all the doors. If they had been Moslem children he would have spoken to them, but since they were Jews he did not see them as children at all—merely as nuisances in his way, like cacti that had to be stepped over carefully because there was no way of going around them. Although he had lived here for almost two years, he did not know the names of any of the Jews. For him they had no names. When he came home and found his door locked, because his brother had gone out and taken both keys with him, he went into any house where the door was open and dropped his bundles on the floor, saying: 'I'll be back in a little while.' He knew they would not touch his property. The Jews were neither friendly nor unfriendly. They too, if they had had money, would have been living in the Spanish end of the town. It made the alley seem less like a Mellah, where only Jews live, to have the two Moslems staying among them.

Salam had the best house in the alley. It was at the end, and its windows gave onto a wilderness of fig trees and cane-brake where squatters had built huts out of thatch and hammered pieces of tin. On the hot nights (for the town was in a plain and the heat stayed in the streets long after the sun had gone) his rooms had a breeze from the south that blew through and out onto the terrace. He was happy with his house and with the life that he and his brother had in it. 'I'm a friend of the world,' he would say. ' A clean heart is better than everything.'

One day he came home and found a small kitten sitting on the terrace. When it saw him it ran to him and purred. He unlocked the door into the kitchen and it went inside. After he had washed his hands and feet in the kitchen he went into his room. The kitten was lying on the mattress, still purring. 'Mimí,' he said to it. He gave it some bread. While it ate the bread it did not stop purring. Bou Ralem came home. He had been drinking beer with some friends in the Café Granada. At first he did not understand why Salam had let the kitten stay. 'It's too young to be worth anything,' he said. 'If it saw a rat it would run and hide.' But when the kitten lay in his lap and played with him he liked it. 'Its name is Mimí,' Salam told him. Nights it slept on the mattress with Salam near his feet. It learned to go down into the alley to relieve itself in the dirt there. The children sometimes tried to catch it, but it ran faster than they did and got to the steps before them, and they did not dare follow it upstairs.

During Ramadan, when they stayed up all night, they moved the mats and cushions and mattresses out on to the terrace and lived out there, talking and laughing until the daylight came. They smoked more kif than usual, and invited their friends home at two in the morning for dinner. Because they were living outside and the kitten could hear them from the alley, it grew bolder and began to visit the canebrake behind the house. It could run very fast, and even if a dog chased it, it could get to the stairs in time. When Salam missed it he would stand up and call to it

over the railing, on one side down the alley and on the other
over the trees and the roofs of the shacks. Sometimes when
he was calling into the alley a Jewish woman would run
out of one of the doors and look at him. He noticed that it
was always the same woman. She would put one hand above
her eyes and stare up at him, and then she would put both
hands on her hips and frown. 'A crazy woman,' he thought,
and he paid no attention to her. One day while he was calling the kitten, the woman shouted up to him in Spanish.
Her voice sounded very angry. *'Oyé!'* she cried, shaking
her arm in the air, 'why are you calling the name of my
daughter?'

Salam kept calling : *'Mimí! Agi! Agiagi, Mimí!'*

The woman moved closer to the steps. She put both hands
above her eyes, but the sun was behind Salam, so that she
could not see him very well. 'You want to insult people?'
she screamed. 'I understand your game. You make fun of
me and my daughter.'

Salam laughed. He put the end of his forefinger to the
side of his head and made circles with it. 'I'm calling my
cat. Who's your daughter?'

'And your cat is called Mimí because you knew my little
girl's name was Mimí. Why don't you behave like civilized
people?'

Salam laughed again and went inside. He did not think
of the woman again. Not many days after that the kitten
disappeared, and no matter how much he called, it did not
come back. He and Bou Ralem went out that night and
searched for it in the canebrake. The moon was bright, and
they found it lying dead, and carried it back to the house
to look at it. Someone had given it a pellet of bread with a
needle inside. Salam sat slowly on the mattress. 'The *Yehou-
día,*' he said.

'You don't know who did it,' Bou Ralem told him.

'It was the *Yehoudia*. Throw me the *mottoui*.' And he began to smoke kif, one pipe after another. Bou Ralem understood that Salam was looking for an answer, and he did not talk. After a while he saw that the time had come to turn off the electricity and light the candle. When he had done this, Salam lay back quietly on the mattress and listened to the dogs barking outside. Now and then he sat up and filled his *sebsi*. Once he passed it to Bou Ralem, and lay back down on the cushions smiling. He had an idea of what he would do. Whe nthey went to bed he said to Bou Ralem : 'She's one mother who's going to wet her pants.'

The next day he got up early and went to the market. In a little stall there he bought several things : a crow's wing, a hundred grams of *jduq jmel* seeds, powdered porcupine quills, some honey, a pressed lizard, and a quarter kilo of *fasoukh*. When he had finished paying for all this he turned away as if he were going to leave the stall, then he said : '*Khaï*, give me another fifty grams of *jduq jmel*.' When the man had weighed the seeds out and put them into a paper and folded it up, he paid him and carried the paper in his left hand as he went on his way home. In the alley the children were throwing clots of mud at one another. They stopped while he went by. The women sat in the doorways with their shawls over their heads. As he passed before the house of the woman who had killed Mimí he let go of the package of *jduq jmel* seeds. Then he went upstairs onto his terrace, walked to the door, and pounded on it. No one answered. He stood in the middle of the terrace where everyone could see him, rubbing his hand over his chin. A minute later he climbed to the terrace next to his and knocked on that door. He handed his parcel to the woman who came to open. 'I left my keys in the market,' he told her. 'I'll be right back.' He ran downstairs, through the alley, and up the street.

Behind the Gailan Garage Bou Ralem was standing. When Salam passed him, he nodded his head once and went along without stopping. Bou Ralem began to walk in the other direction, back to the house. As he opened the gate on to the terrace, the woman from next door called to him. 'Haven't you seen your brother? He left his keys in the market.' 'No,' Bou Ralem said, and went in, leaving the door open. He sat down and smoked a cigarette while he waited. In a little while the talking in the alley below sounded louder. He stood up and went to the door to listen. A woman was crying: 'It's *jduq jmel!* Mimí had it in her hand!' Soon there were many more voices, and the woman from the next terrace ran downstairs in her bathrobe, carrying a parcel. 'That's it,' Bou Ralem said to himself. When she arrived the shouting grew louder. He listened for a time, smiling. He went out and ran downstairs. They were all in the alley outside the woman's door, and the little girl was inside the house, screaming. Without looking toward them he ran by on the far side of the alley.

Salem was inside the café, drinking a glass of tea. 'Sit down,' he told Bou Ralem. 'I'm not going to get Fatma Daifa before eleven.' He ordered his brother a tea. 'Were they making a lot of noise?' he asked him. Bou Ralem nodded his head. Salem smiled. 'I'd like to hear them,' he said. 'You'll hear them,' Bou Ralem told him. 'They're not going to stop.'

At eleven o'clock they left the café and went through the back passages of the Medina to Fatma Daifa's house. She was the sister of their mother's mother, and thus not of their family, so that they did not feel it was shameful to use her in the game. She was waiting for them at the door, and together they went back to Salam's house.

The old woman went into the alley ahead of Salam and Bou Ralem, and walked straight to the door where all the women were gathered. She held her *haik* tightly around her head so that no part of her face showed, except one eye. She pushed against the Jewish women and held out one hand. 'Give me my things,' she told them. She did not bother to speak Spanish with them because she knew they understood Arabic. 'You have my things.' They did have them and they were still looking at them, but then they turned to look at her. She seized all the packages and put them into her *kouffa* quickly. 'No shame!' she shouted at the women. 'Go and look after your children.' She pushed the other way and went back into the alley where Salem and Bou Ralem stood waiting. The three went upstairs and into Salam's house, and they shut the door. They had lunch there and stayed all day, talking and laughing. When everyone had gone to bed, Salam took Fatma Daifa home.

The next day the Jews all stared at them when they went out, but no one said anything to them. The woman Salam had wanted to frighten did not come to her door at all, and the little girl was not in the alley playing with the other children. It was clear that the Jews thought Fatma Daifa had put a spell on the child. They would not have believed Salam and Bou Ralem alone could do such a thing, but they knew a Moslem woman had the power. The two brothers were very much pleased with the joke. It is forbidden to practice magic, but the old woman was their witness that they had not done such a thing. She had taken home all the packages just as they had been when she had snatched them away from the Jewish women, and she had promised to keep them that way, so that in case of trouble she could prove that nothing had been used.

The Jewish woman went to the *comisaría* to complain. She found a young policeman sitting at his desk listening to a small radio he had in his hand, and she began to tell him that the Moslems in her *haouma* had bought charms to use against her daughter. The policeman did not like her, partly because she was Jewish and spoke Spanish instead of Arabic, and partly because he did not approve of people who believed in magic, but he listened politely until she said: 'That Moslem is a *sinvergüenza*.' She tried to go on to say that there were many very good Moslems, but he did not like her words. He frowned at the woman and said: 'Why do you say all this? What makes you think they put a spell on your little girl?' She told him how the three had shut themselves in all day with the packages of bad things from the market. The policeman looked at her in surprise. 'And for a dead lizard you came all the way here?' he laughed. He sent her away and went on listening to his radio.

The people in the alley still did not speak to Salam and Bou Ralem, and the little girl did not come out to play in the mud with the others. When the woman went to the market she took her with her. 'Hold on to my skirt,' she would tell her. But one day in front of the service station the child let go of the woman's skirt for a minute. When she ran to catch up with her mother, she fell and her knee hit a broken bottle. The woman saw the blood and began to scream. People stopped walking. In a few minutes a Jew came by and helped the woman carry the child to a pharmacy. They bandaged the little girl's knee and the woman took her home. Then she went back to the pharmacy to get her baskets, but on the way she stopped at the police station. She found the same policeman sitting at his desk.

'If you want to see the proof of what I told you, come and look at my little girl now,' she told him. 'Again?' said the policeman. He was not friendly with her, but he took her name and address, and later that day on his way home he called at her house. He looked at the little girl's knee and tickled her ribs so that she laughed. 'All children fall down,' he said. 'But who is this Moslem? Where does he live?' The mother showed him the stairs at the end of the alley. He did not intend to speak with Salam, but he wanted to finish with the woman once and for all. He went out into the alley, and saw that the woman was watching him from the door, so he walked slowly to the foot of the stairs. When he had decided she was no longer looking, he started to go. At that moment he heard a voice behind him. He turned and saw Salam standing above him on the terrace. He did not much like his face, and he told himself that if he ever saw him in the street he would have a few words with him.

One morning Salam went early to the market to get fresh kif. When he found it he bought three hundred francs' worth. As he went out through the gates into the street the policeman, who was waiting for him, stopped him. 'I want to speak with you,' he told him. Salam stretched his fingers tightly around the kif in his pocket. 'Is everything all right?' said the policeman. 'Everything is fine,' Salam replied. 'No trouble?' the policeman insisted, looking at him as if he knew what Salam had just bought. Salam answered: 'No trouble.' The policeman said: 'See that it stays like that.' Salam was angry at being spoken to in this way for no reason, but with the kif in his pocket he could only be thankful that he was not being searched. 'I'm a friend of the world,' he said, trying to smile. The policeman did not answer, and turned away.

'A very bad thing,' thought Salam as he hurried home

with the kif. No policeman had bothered him before this. When he reached his room he wondered if he should hide the package under a tile in the floor, but he decided that if he did that, he himself would be living like a Jew, who each time there is a knock at the door ducks his head and trembles. He spread the kif out on the table defiantly and left it there. During the afternoon he and Bou Ralem cut it. He did not mention the policeman, but he was thinking of him all the time they were working. When the sun had gone down behind the plain and the soft breeze began to come in through the windows he took off his shirt and lay back on the pillows to smoke. Bou Ralem filled his *mottoui* with the fresh kif and went out to a café. 'I'm staying here,' said Salam.

He smoked for an hour or more. It was a hot night. The dogs had begun to bark in the canebrake. A woman and a man in one of the huts below were cursing one another. Sometimes the woman stopped shouting and merely screamed. The sound bothered Salam. He could not be happy. He got up and dressed, took his *sebsi* and his *mottoui*, and went out. Instead of turning toward the town when he left the alley, he walked toward the highway. He wanted to sit in a quiet place in order to find out what to do. If the policeman had not suspected him, he would not have stopped him. Since he had stopped him once, he might do it again, and the next time he might search him. 'That's not freedom,' he said to himself. A few cars went by. Their headlights made the tree-trunks yellow as they passed. After each car had gone, there was only the blue light of the moon and the sky. When he got to the bridge over the river, he climbed down the bank under the girders, and went along a path to a rock that hung out high above the water. There he sat and looked over the edge at the deep muddy river that was moving below in the moonlight. He felt the kif in his head, and he knew he was going to make it work for him.

He put the plan together slowly. It was going to cost a thousand francs, but he had that, and he was willing to spend it. After six pipes, when he had everything arranged in his mind, he stuffed his *sebsi* into his pocket, jumped up, and climbed the path to the highway. He walked back to the town quickly, going into the Medina by a dirt road where the houses had gardens, and where behind the walls all along the way there were dogs barking at the moon. Not many people walked at night in this part of the town. He went to the house of his cousin Abdallah, who was married to a woman from Sidi Kacem. The house was never empty. Two or three of her brothers were always there with their families. Salam spoke privately with Abdallah in the street outside the door, asking for one of the brothers whose face was not known in the town. Abdallah went in and quickly came out again with someone. The man had a beard, wore a country *djellaba*, and carried his shoes in his hand. They spoke together for a few minutes. 'Go with him,' said Abdallah, when thye had finished talking. Salam and the bearded man said goodnight to Abdallah and went away.

At Salam's house that night the man slept on a mat in the kitchen. When morning came, they washed and had coffee and pastries. While they were eating Salam took out his thousand-franc note and put it into an envelope. On the outside of it Bou Ralem had printed the word GRACIAS in pencil. Soon Salam and the man from the country got up and went out through the town until they came to a side street opposite the back entrance of the police station. There they stood against the wall and talked. 'You don't know his name,' said the man. 'We don't have to,' Salam told him. 'When he comes out and gets into one of the cars and drives away, you run over to the office and give them the envelope, and say you tried to catch him before he left.' He waved the envelope in his hand. 'Ask them to give this to him when he comes back. They'll take it.'

'He may walk,' said the man. 'Then what will I do?'

'The police never walk,' Salam said. 'You'll see. Then you run out again. This street is the best one. Keep going, that's all. I won't be here. I'll see you at Abdallah's.'

They waited a long time. The sun grew hotter and they moved into the shade of a fig tree, always watching the door of the *comisaría* from where they stood. Several policemen came out, and for each one the man from the country was ready to run, but Salam held on to him and said : 'No, no, no !' When the policeman they were waiting for finally did stand in the doorway, Salam drew in his breath and whispered : 'There he is. Wait till he drives off, then run.' He turned away and walked very fast down the street into the Medina.

When the man from the country had explained clearly who the envelope was for, he handed it to the policeman at the desk, said, 'Thank you,' and ran out quickly. The policeman looked at the envelope, then tried to call him back, but he had gone. Since all messages which came for any of the policemen had to be put on the captain's desk first, he sent the envelope in to his office. The captain held it up to the light. When the policeman came back he called him in and made him open it in front of him. 'Who is it from?' said the captain. The policeman scratched his head. He could not answer. 'I see,' said the captain. The next week he had the man transferred. Word came from the capital that he was to be sent to Rissani. 'See how many friends you can make in the desert,' the captain told him. He would not listen to anything the policeman tried to say.

Salam went to Tangier. When he returned he heard that the policeman had been sent to the Sahara. This made him laugh a great deal. He went to the market and bought a half-grown goat. Then he invited Fatma Daifa and Abdallah and his wife and two of the brothers with their wives and children, and they killed the goat and ate it. It was nearly dawn by the time they all went home. Fatma Daifa did not want to go through the streets alone, and since Salam and Bou Ralem were too drunk to take her, she slept in the kitchen on the floor. When she woke up it was late, but Salam and Bou Ralem were still asleep. She got her things together, put on her *haïk* and went out. As she came to the house of the woman with the little girl, she stood still and looked in. The woman saw her and was frightened. 'What do you want?' she cried. Fatma Daifa knew she was meddling, but she thought this was the right thing to do for Salam. She pretended not to see the woman's frightened face, and she shook her fist back at the terrace, crying into the air : 'Now I see what sort of man you are ! You think you can cheat me? Listen to me ! None of it's going to work, do you hear?' She walked on down the alley shouting : 'None of it !' The other Jewish women came and stood around the door and sat on the curb in front of it. They agreed that if the old woman had fought with the two men there was no more danger from the magic, because only the old woman had the power to make it work. The mother of the little girl was happy, and the next day the child was playing in the mud with the others.

Salam went in and out of the alley as always, not noticing the children or the people. It was half a month before he said one day to Bou Ralem : 'I think the Jews are feel-

ing better. I saw the wrong Mimí out loose this morning.'
He was free again now that the policeman was gone, and
he could carry his kif in his pocket without worrying when
he went out through the streets to the café. The next time
he saw Fatma Daifa she asked him about the Jews in his
alley. 'It's finished. They've forgotten,' he said. 'Good,' she
replied. Then she went to her house and got out the porcupine quill powder and the crow's wing and the seeds and
all the rest of the packages. She put them into her basket,
carried them to the market, and sold them there, and with
the money she bought bread, oil, and eggs. She went home
and cooked her dinner.

The Wind at Beni Midar

At Beni Midar there is a barracks. It has many rows of small buildings, whitewashed, and everything is in the middle of big rocks, on the side of the mountain behind the town. A quiet place when the wind is not blowing. A few Spanish still live in the houses along the road. They run the shops. But now the people in the street are Moslems, mountain men with goats and sheep, or soldiers from the *cuartel* looking for wine. The Spanish sell wine to men they know. One Jew sells it to almost anybody. But there never is enough wine in the town for everybody who wants it. Beni Midar has only one street, that comes down out of the mountains, curves back and forth like a snake between the houses for a while, and goes on, back into the mountains. Sunday is a bad day, the one free time the soldiers have, when they can walk back and forth all day between the shops and houses. A few Spaniards in black clothes go into the church at the hour when the Rhmara ride their donkeys out of the *souk*. Later the Spaniards come out of the church and go home. Nothing else happens because all the shops are shut. There is nothing the soldiers can buy.

Driss had been stationed for eight months in Beni Midar. Because the *cabran* in charge of his unit had been a neighbor of his in Tetuan, he was not unhappy. The *cabran* had a friend with a motorcycle. Together they went each month to Tetuan. There the *cabran* always saw Driss's sister, who

142

made a big bundle of food to send back to the barracks for him. She sent him chickens and cakes, cigarettes and figs, and always many hard-boiled eggs. He shared the eggs with two or three friends, and did not complain about being in Beni Midar.

Not even the brothels were open on Sunday. It was the day when everyone walked from one end of the town to the other, back and forth, many times. Sometimes Driss walked like this with his friends. Usually he took his gun and went down into the valley to hunt for hares. When he came back at twilight he stopped in a small café at the edge of the town and had a glass of tea and a few pipes of kif. If it had not been the only café he would never have gone into it. Shameful things happened there. Several times he had seen men from the mountains get up from the mat and do dances that left blood on the floor. These men were Djilala, and no one thought of stopping them, not even Driss. They did not dance because they wanted to dance, and it was this that made him angry and ashamed. It seemed to him that the world should be made in such a way that a man is free to dance or not as he feels. A Djilali can do only what the music tells him to do. When the musicians, who are Djilala too, play the music that has the power, his eyes shut and he falls on the floor. And until the man has shown the proof and tasted his own blood, the musicians do not begin the music that will bring him back to the world. They should do something about it, Driss said to the other soldiers who went with him to the café, and they agreed.

He had talked about it with his *cabran* in the public garden. The *cabran* said that when all the children in the land were going to school every day there would be no more *djenoun*. Women would no longer be able to put spells on their husbands. And the Djilala and the Hamatcha and all the others would stop cutting their legs and arms and chests. Driss thought about this for a long time. He was glad to hear that the government knew about these bad things. 'But if they know,' he thought, 'why don't they do something now? The day they get every one of the children in school I'll be lying beside Sidi Ali el Mandri.' He was thinking of the cemetery at Bab Sebta in Tetuan. When he saw the *cabran* again he said : 'If they can do something about it, they ought to do it now.' The *cabran* did not seem interested. 'Yes,' he said.

When Driss got his permission and went home he told his father what the *cabran* had said. 'You mean the government thinks it can kill all evil spirits?' his father cried.

'That's right. It can,' said Driss. 'It's going to.'

His father was old and had no confidence in the young men who now ran the government. 'It's impossible,' he said. 'They should let them alone. Leave them under their stones. Children have gone to school before, and how many were hurt by *djenoun?* But if the government begins to make trouble for them, you'll see what will happen. They'll go after the children first.'

Driss had expected his father to speak this way, but when he heard the words he was ashamed. He did not answer. Some of his friends were without respect for God. They ate during Ramadan and argued with their fathers. He was glad not to be like them. But he felt that his father was wrong.

One hot summer Sunday when the sky was very blue Driss lay in bed late. The men who slept in his room at the barracks had gone out. He listened to the radio. 'It would be good down in the valley on a day like this,' he thought. He saw himself swimming in one of the big pools, and he thought of the hot sun on his back afterward. He got up

and unlocked the cupboard to look at his gun. Even before
he took it out he said, '*Yah latif!*' because he remembered
that he had only one cartridge left, and it was Sunday. He
slammed the cupboard door shut and got back into bed.
The radio began to give the news. He sat up, spat as far out
as he could from the bed, and turned it off. In the silence
he heard many birds singing in the *safsaf* tree outside the
window. He scratched his head. Then he got up and dressed.
In the courtyard he saw Mehdi going toward the stairs.
Mehdi was on his way to do sentry duty in the box outside
the main gate.

'*Khaï!* Does four rials sound good to you?'

Mehdi looked at him. 'Is this number sixty, three, fifty-
one?' This was the name of an Egyptian song that came
over the radio nearly every day. The song ended with the
word nothing. Nothing, nothing, sung over and over again.

'Why not?' As they walked along together, Driss moved
closer, so that his thigh rubbed against Mehdi's.

'The price is ten, *khoya*.'

'With all its cartridges?'

'You want me to open it up and show you here?' Mehdi's
voice was angry. The words came out of the side of his
mouth.

Driss said nothing. They came to the top of the stairs.
Mehdi was walking fast. 'You'll have to have it back here
by seven,' he said. 'Do you want it?'

In his head Driss saw the long day in the empty town.
'Yes,' he said. 'Stay there.' He hurried back to the room,
unlocked his cupboard, and took out his gun. From the shelf
he pulled down his pipe, his kif, and a loaf of bread. He put
his head outside the door. There was no one in the courtyard but Mehdi sitting on the wall at the other end. Then
with the old gun in his hands he ran all the way to Mehdi.

Mehdi took it and went down the stairs, leaving his own gun lying on the wall. Driss took up the gun, waited a moment, and followed him. When he went past the sentry box he heard Mehdi's voice say softly : 'I need the ten at seven, *khoya*.'

Driss grunted. He knew how dark it was in there. No officer ever stuck his head inside the door on Sundays. Ten rials, he thought, and he's running no risk. He looked around at the goats among the rocks. The sun was hot, but the air smelled sweet, and he was happy to be walking down the side of the mountain. He pulled the visor of his cap further down over his eyes and began to whistle. Soon he came out in front of the town, below it on the other side of the valley. He could see the people on the benches in the park at the top of the cliff, small but clear and black. They were Spaniards and they were waiting for the bell of their church to begin to ring.

He got to the highest pool about the time the sun was overhead. When he lay on the rocks afterward eating his bread, the sun burned him. No animals will move before three, he thought. He put his trousers on and crawled into the shade of the oleander bushes to sleep. When he awoke the air was cooler. He smoked all the kif he had, and went walking through the valley. Sometimes he sang. He found no hares, and so he put small stones on the tops of the rocks and fired at them. Then he climbed back up the other side of the valley and followed the highway into the town.

He came to the café and went in. The musicians were playing an *aaita* and singing. The tea drinkers clapped their hands with the music. A soldier cried : 'Driss ! Sit down !' He sat with his friends and smoked some of their kif. Then he bought four rials' worth from the cutter who sat on the platform with the musicians, and went on smoking. 'Nothing was moving in the valley today,' he told them. 'It was dead down there.'

A man with a yellow turban on his head who sat nearby closed his eyes and fell against the man next to him. The others around him moved to a further part of the mat. The man toppled over and lay on the floor.

'Another one?' cried Driss. 'They should stay in Djebel Habib. I can't look at him.'

The man took a long time to get to his feet. His arms and legs had been captured by the drums, but his body was fighting, and he groaned. Driss tried to pay not attention to him. He smoked his pipe and looked at his friends, pretending that no Djilali was in front of him. When the man pulled out his knife he could not pretend any longer. He watched the blood running into the man's eyes. It made a blank red curtain over each hole. The man opened his eyes wider, as if he wanted to see through the blood. The drums were loud.

Driss got up and paid the *qahouaji* for his tea. He said good-bye to the others and went out. The sun would soon go below the top of the mountain. Its light made him want to shut his eyes, because he had a lot of kif in his head. He walked through the town to the higher end and turned into a lane that led up into another valley. In this place there was no one. Cacti grew high on each side of the lane, and the spiders had built a world of webs between their thorns. Because he walked fast, the kif began to boil in his head. Soon he was very hungry, but all the fruit had been picked from the cacti along the lane. He came to a small farmhouse with a thatched roof. Behind it on the empty mountainside there were more cacti still pink with hundreds of *hindiyats*. A dog in a shed beside the house began to bark. There was no sign of people. He stood still for a while and listened to the dog. Then he walked toward the cactus patch. He was sure no one was in the house. Many years ago his sister had shown him how to pick *hindiyats* without letting the needles get into the flesh of his hands. He laid his gun on the ground behind a low stone wall and began to gather the fruit. As he picked he saw in his head the two blind red holes of the Djilali's eyes, and under his breath he cursed all Djilala. When he had a great pile of fruit on the ground he sat down and began to eat, throwing the peels over his shoulder. As he ate he grew hungrier, and so he picked more. The picture he had in his head of the man's face shiny with blood slowly faded. He thought only of the *hindiyats* he was eating. It was almost dark there on the mountainside. He looked at his watch and jumped up, because he remembered that Mehdi had to have his gun at seven o'clock. In the dim light he could not see the gun anywhere. He searched behind the wall, where he thought he had laid it, but he saw only stones and bushes.

'It's gone, *Allah istir*,' he said. His heart pounded. He ran back to the lane and stood there a while. The dog barked without stopping.

It was dark before he reached the gate of the barracks. Another man was in the sentry box. The *cabran* was waiting for him in the room. The old gun Driss's father had given him lay on his bed.

'Do you know where Mehdi is?' the *cabran* asked him.

'No,' said Driss.

'He's in the dark house, the son of a whore. And do you know why?'

Driss sat down on the bed. The *cabran* is my friend, he was thinking. 'It's gone,' he said, and told him how he had laid the gun on the ground, and a dog had been barking, and no one had come by, and still it had disappeared. 'Maybe the dog was a *djinn*,' he said when he had finished. He did not really believe the dog had anything to do with it, but he could not think of anything else to say then.

The *cabran* looked at him a long time and said nothing. He shook his head. 'I thought you had some brains,' he said at last. Then his face grew very angry, and he pulled Driss out into the courtyard and told a soldier to lock him up.

At ten o'clock that night he went to see Driss. He found him smoking his *sebsi* in the dark. The cell was full of kif smoke. 'Garbage!' cried the *cabran*, and he took the pipe and the kif away from him. 'Tell the truth,' he said to Driss. 'You sold the gun, didn't you?'

'On my mother's head, it's just as I told you! There was only the dog.'

The *cabran* could not make him say anything different. He slammed the door and went to the café in the town to have a glass of tea. He sat listening to the music, and he began to smoke the kif he had taken from Driss. If Driss was telling the truth, then it was only the kif in Driss's head that had made him lose the gun, and in that case there was a chance that it could be found.

The *cabran* had not smoked in a long time. As the kif filled his head he began to be hungry, and he remembered the times when he had been a boy smoking kif with his friends. Always they had gone to look for *hindiyats* afterward, because they tasted better than anything else and cost nothing. They always knew where there were some growing. 'A *kouffa* full of good *hindiyats*,' he thought. He shut his eyes and went on thinking.

The next morning early the *cabran* went out and stood on a high rock behind the barracks, looking carefully all around the valley and the bare mountainside. Not far away he saw a lane with cacti along it, and further up there was a whole forest of cactus. 'There,' he said to himself.

He walked among the rocks until he came to the lane, and he followed the lane to the farmhouse. The dog began to bark. A woman came to the doorway and looked at him. He paid no attention to her, but went straight to the high cacti on the hillside behind the house. There were many *hindiyats* still to be eaten, but the *cabran* did not eat any of them. He had no kif in his head and he was thinking only of the gun. Beside a stone wall there was a big pile of *hindiya* peelings. Someone had eaten a great many. Then he saw the sun shining on part of the gun's barrel under the peelings. 'Hah!' he shouted, and he seized the gun and wiped it all over with his handkerchief. On his way back to the barracks he felt so happy that he decided to play a joke on Driss.

He hid the gun under his bed. With a glass of tea and a piece of bread in his hand he went to see Driss. He found him asleep on the floor in the dark.

'Daylight is here!' he shouted. He laughed and kicked Driss's foot to wake him up. Driss sat on the floor drinking the tea and the *cabran* stood in the doorway scratching his chin. He looked down at the floor, but not at Driss. After a time he said : 'Last night you told me a dog was barking?'

Driss was certain the *cabran* was going to make fun of him. He was sorry he had mentioned the dog. 'Yes,' he said, not sounding sure.

'If it was the dog,' the *cabran* went on, I know how to get it back. You have to help me.'

Driss looked up at him. He could not believe the *cabran* was being serious. Finally he said in a low voice : 'I was joking when I said that. I had kif in my head.'

The *cabran* was angry. 'You think it's a joke to lose a

gun that belongs to the Sultan? You did sell it! You haven't got kif in your head now. Maybe you can tell the truth. He stepped toward Driss, and Driss thought he was going to hit him. He stood up quickly. 'I told you the truth,' he said. 'It was gone.'

The *cabran* rubbed his chin and looked down at the floor again for a minute. 'The next time a Djilali begins to dance in the café, we'll do it,' he told him. He shut the door and left Driss alone.

Two days later the *cabran* came again to the dark house. He had another soldier with him. 'Quick!' he told Driss. 'There's one dancing now.'

They went out into the courtyard and Driss blinked his eyes. 'Listen,' said the *cabran*. 'When the Djilali is drinking his own blood he has power. What you have to do is ask him to make the *djinn* bring me the gun. I'm going to sit in my room and burn *djaoui*. That may help.'

'I'll do it,' said Driss. 'But it won't do any good.'

The other soldier took Driss to the café. The Djilali was a tall man from the mountains. He had already taken out his knife, and he was waving it in the air. The soldier made Driss sit down near the musicians, and then he waited until the man began to lick the blood from his arms. Then, because he thought he might be sick if he watched any longer, Driss raised his right arm toward the Djilali and said in a low voice: 'In the name of Allah, *khoya*, make the *djinn* that stole Mehdi's gun take it now to Aziz the *cabran*.' The Djilali seemed to be staring at him, but Driss could not be sure whether he had heard his words or not.

The soldier took him back to the barracks. The *cabran* was sitting under a plum tree beside the kitchen door. He told the soldier to go away and jumped up. 'Come,' he said, and he led Driss to the room. The air was blue with the

smoke of the *djaoui* he had been burning. He pointed to
the middle of the floor. 'Look!' he cried. A gun was lying
there. Driss ran and picked it up. After he had looked at it
carefully, he said : 'It's the gun.' And his voice was full of
fear. The *cabran* could see that Driss had not been sure the
thing was possible, but that now he no longer had any
doubt.

The *cabran* was happy to have fooled him so easily. He
laughed. 'You see, it worked,' he said. 'It's lucky for you.
Mehdi's going to be in the dark house for another week.'

Driss did not answer. He felt even worse than when he
had been watching the Djilali slicing the flesh of his arms.

That night he lay in bed worrying. It was the first time
he had had anything to do with a *djinn* or an *affrit*. Now
he had entered into their world. It was a dangerous world
and he did not trust the *cabran* any longer. 'What am I going to do?' thought. The men all around him were sleeping, but he could not close his eyes. Soon he got up and
stepped outside. The leaves of the *safsaf* tree were hissing
in the wind. On the other side of the courtyard there was
light in one of the windows. Some of the officers were talking there. He walked slowly around the garden in the middle
and looked up at the sky, thinking of how different his life
was going to be now. As he came near the lighted window
he heard a great burst of laughter. The *cabran* was telling a
story. Driss stopped walking and listened.

'And he said to the Djilali : "Please, sidi, would you ask
the dog that stole my gun—"'

The men laughed again, and the sound covered the
cabran's voice.

He went quickly back and got into bed. If they knew he
had heard the *cabran's* story they would laugh even more.
He lay in the bed thinking, and he felt poison come into

his heart. It was the *cabran's* fault that the *djinn* had been called, and now in front of his superior officers he was pretending that he had had nothing to do with it. Later the *cabran* came in and went to bed, and it was quiet in the courtyard, but Driss lay thinking for a long time before he went to sleep.

In the days that came after that, the *cabran* was friendly again, but Driss did not want to see him smile. He thought with hatred : 'In his head I'm afraid of him now because he knows how to call a *djinn*. He jokes with me now because he has power.'

He could not laugh or be happy when the *cabran* was nearby. Each night he lay awake for a long time after the others had gone to sleep. He listened to the wind moving the hard leaves of the *safsaf* tree, and he thought only of how he could break the *cabran's* power.

When Mehdi came out of the dark house he spoke against the *cabran*. Driss paid him his ten rials. 'A lot of money for ten days in the dark house.' Mehdi grumbled, and he looked at the bill in his hand. Driss pretended not to understand. 'He's a son of a whore,' he said.

Mehdi snorted. 'And you have the head of a needle,' he said. 'It all came from you. The wind blows the kif out your ears !'

'You think I wasn't in the dark house too ?' cried Driss. But he could not tell Mehdi about the Djilali and the dog. 'He's a son of a whore,' he said again.

Mehdi's eyes grew narrow and stiff. 'I'll do his work for him. He'll think he's in the dark house himself when I finish.'

Mehdi went on his way. Driss stood watching him go.

The next Sunday Driss got up early and walked into Beni Midar. The *souk* was full of rows of mountain people in white clothes. He walked in among the donkeys and climbed

the steps to the stalls. There he went to see an old man who
sold incense and herbs. People called him El Fqih. He sat
down in front of El Fqih and said : 'I want something for a
son of a whore.'

El Fqih looked at him angrily. 'A sin!' He raised his
forefinger and shook it back and forth. 'Sins are not my
work.' Driss did not say anything. El Fqih spoke more
quietly now. 'To balance that, it is said that each trouble
in the world has its remedy. There are cheap remedies and
remedies that cost a lot of money.' He stopped.

Driss waited. 'How much is this one?' he asked him. The
old man was not pleased because he wanted to talk longer.
But he said : 'I'll give you a name for five rials.' He looked
sternly at Driss, leaned forward and whispered a name in
his ear. 'In the alley behind the sawmill,' he said aloud.
'The blue tin shack with the canebrake in back of it.' Driss
paid him and ran down the steps.

He found the house. The old woman stood in the doorway with a checked tablecloth over her head. Her eyes had
turned white like milk. They looked to Driss like the eyes of
an old dog. He said : 'You're Anisa?'

'Come into the house,' she told him. It was almost dark
inside. He told her he wanted something to break the power
of a son of a whore. 'Give me ten rials now,' she said. 'Come
back at sunset with another ten. It will be ready.'

After the midday meal he went out into the courtyard.
He met Mehdi and asked him to go with him to the café in
Beni Midar. They walked through the town in the hot afternoon sun. It was still early when they got to the café, and
there was plenty of space on the mats. They sat in a dark
corner. Driss took out his kif and his *sebsi* and they smoked.
When the musicians began to play, Mehdi said : 'The circus
is back!' But Driss did not want to talk about the Djilala.

He talked about the *cabran*. He gave the pipe many times to Mehdi, and he watched Mehdi growing more angry with the *cabran* as he smoked. He was not surprised when Mehdi cried : 'I'll finish it tonight !'

'No, *khoya*,' said Driss. 'You don't know. He's gone way up. He's a friend of all the officers now. They bring him bottles of wine.'

'He'll come down,' Mehdi said. 'Before dinner tonight. In the courtyard. You be there and watch it.'

Driss handed him the pipe and paid for the tea. He left Mehdi there and went into the street to walk up and down because he did not want to sit still any longer. When the sky was red behind the mountain he went to the alley by the sawmill. The old woman was in the doorway.

'Come in,' she said as before. When they were inside the room she handed him a paper packet. 'He has to take all of it,' she said. She took the money and pulled at his sleeve. 'I never saw you,' she said. 'Good-bye.'

Driss went to his room and listened to the radio. When dinner time came he stood inside the doorway looking out into the courtyard. In the shadows at the other end he thought he could see Mehdi, but he was not sure. There were many soldiers walking around in the courtyard, waiting for dinner. Soon there was shouting near the top of the steps. The soldiers began to run toward the other end of the courtyard. Driss looked from the doorway and saw only the running soldiers. He called to the men in the room. 'Something's happening !' They all ran out. Then with the paper of powder in his hand he went back into the room to the *cabran's* bed and lifted up the bottle of wine one of the officers had given the *cabran* the day before. It was almost full. He pulled out the cork and let the powder slide into the bottle. He shook the bottle and put the cork back.

There was still shouting in the courtyard. He ran out. When he got near the crowd, he saw Mehdi being dragged along the ground by three soldiers. He was kicking. The *cabran* sat on the wall with his head down, holding his arm. There was blood all over his face and shirt.

It was almost a half-hour before the *cabran* came to eat his dinner. His face was covered with bruises and his arm was bandaged and hung in a sling. Mehdi had cut it with his knife at the last minute when the soldiers had begun to pull them apart. The *cabran* did not speak much, and the men did not try to talk with him. He sat on his bed and ate. While he was eating he drank all the wine in the bottle.

That night the *cabran* moaned in his sleep. A dry wind blew between the mountains. It made a great noise in the *safsaf* tree outside the window. The air roared and the leaves rattled, but Driss still heard the *cabran's* voice crying. In the morning the doctor came to look at him. The *cabran's* eyes were open but he could not see. And his mouth was open but he could not speak. They carried him out of the room where the soldiers lived and put him somewhere else. 'Maybe the power is broken now,' thought Driss.

A few days later a truck came to the barracks, and he saw two men carrying the *cabran* on a stretcher to the truck. Then he was sure that the *cabran's* soul had been torn out of his body and that the power was truly broken. In his head he made a prayer of thanks to Allah. He stood with some other soldiers on a rock above the barracks watching the truck grow smaller as it moved down the mountain.

'It's bad for me,' he told a man who stood nearby. 'He always brought me food from home.' The soldier shook his head.

ARENA

'The work of a master, and a master not only of language and comedy but of feeling too'.

Sunday Times

RATES OF EXCHANGE
Malcolm Bradbury

Dr Petworth is not, it had better be admitted, a person of any great interest at all. He is white and male, forty and married, bourgeois and British — all items to anyone's contemporary discredit. He is a man to whom life has been kind, and he has paid the price for it. He teaches; that is what he does. He is also a practised cultural traveller, a man who has had diarrhoea for the British Council in almost all parts of the civilized or part-civilized world. And that is why he is here now, in the summer of 1981, in the capital city of a small dark nation known in all the history books as the bloody battlefield of central eastern Europe, travelling culturally. And preparing, though he doesn't know it — to lose more than his luggage.

'A brilliant *tour de force* ... Superb entertainment with an underpinning of reflection and observation that makes you want instantly to read the book again'

Sunday Telegraph

'Some of the liveliest contemporary writing'

Guardian

ARENA

KOKORO

Natsume Soseki

When the old values meet the new in Japan

In Tokyo a lonely young student from the provinces is befriended by a sophisticated older man. Yet the man himself is lonely too. For a dark shadow from his past makes him feel like a mummy left in the midst of living beings. Even the man's wife has never penetrated this tragic mystery.

Then one day the student is dramatically taken into his mentor's confidence . . .

In this beautiful, evocative portrait of Japan at the turn of the century, Natsume Soseki explores the tragic conflicts between old and new, love and duty, friendship and self-interest.

Natsume Soseki is regarded as the greatest novelist of the Meiji era, when Japan began to blend Western culture with oriental traditions.

'One of the most important Japanese writers of the modern period'   *The Times Literary Supplement*

'Exquisite. The novel represents the moment at which the limitations and gifts of the native genius triumphed over an alien literature' *New York Times*